Knud Romer was born in 1960 in Funen, in Denmark,
it matters so small that it is over before it starts. When not
writing, he acts. His credits include The Idiots by Lars von
Trier and Allegro by Christopher Boe.

NOTHING BUT FEAR

Knud Romer

Translated by John Mason

A complete catalogue record for this book can be obtained from the British Library on request

The right of Knud Romer to be identified as the author of this work has been asserted by him in accordance with the Copyright, Designs and Patents Act 1988

First published as *Den Som Blinker Er Bange For Dodenx* in 2006 by Aschehoug Forlag, Copenhagen, Denmark

First published in 2012 by Serpent's Tail,
an imprint of Profile Books Ltd
3A Exmouth House
Pine Street
London EC1R 0JH
website: www.serpentstail.com

ISBN 978 1 84668 714 3
eISBN 1 84765 642 1

Designed and typeset by sue@lambledesign.demon.co.uk
Printed and bound by CPI Group (UK)
Ltd, Croydon, CR0 4YY

10 9 8 7 6 5 4 3 2 1

I feared my grandfather. Always nothing but fear. I knew him only as Papa Schneider. What else they called him, what his Christian name was I had no idea. It made no difference anyway, since I wouldn't have dreamt of calling him by his first name. He was not a man you were on first-name terms with.

Papa Schneider had miles of scar on his face, all on his left cheek. They were duelling scars from the century before last, when he had been a member of a *Schlägerverein*. Members of the club would take it in turns to defend their honour by laying about each other with their sabres – their faces not moving a muscle, their left arm tucked behind their back.

He had grey-black, swept back hair and a high forehead, and to look him in the eye was to challenge him: *Sie haben mich fixiert, mein Herr!* He was beady-eyed, his gaze directed only outwards, and I don't know if anyone ever met it without living to regret it. Except Grandmother – and that's what made her great. She could look Papa Schneider in the eye – my mother never could – but she was the only one, his soft spot, hidden from everyone, while the rest of him was hard and impregnable.

He ruled supreme from the head of the table at my mother and father's house, where his picture hung on the wall of the dining room. It had a gold frame and in it you could see a clearing in a woodland landscape. Papa Schneider was sitting in the grass with a book, gazing straight ahead. Grandmother was at his side with a baby in her arms, and my mother was the little girl holding their hunting dog, Bello. With book, baby and Bello each had been given their role. Papa Schneider was spirit and culture, the woman stood for childbirth, and the children were closer to nature and more akin to dogs that had to be trained.

When we ate, I sat straight as a ramrod on my chair with both hands on the table and my napkin tucked under my chin, as though Papa Schneider were sitting at table with us keeping an eye on me. If I made a false move – cut a potato with my knife or spoke without being spoken to – he would plunge a fork into my hand, I knew he would.

Papa Schneider was the strictest person I have ever known and was everything that is stiff and hard and hurts. He was the top button of your shirt. He was the teeth of the comb when you were being wet-combed. He was every grazed knee, he was the fear of being late. No, I was not on first-name terms with him – and nor was anyone else.

I don't think anyone knew what his name was, or even thought about it. My Grandfather was alone in carrying it around inside him like a terrible secret – and the wildest of gambles. For if one day he heard it, he heard himself called by his Christian name, he would know whose voice it was. No one knew it apart from him – no one but God.

During the war my Grandmother – my mother's mother – exploded in a cellar full of white gas. Her name was Damaris Dora Renata Matthes and she had been one of the loveliest women in Germany. She was as beautiful as a Greek statue, Mother always said, and, sitting and looking at photographs of her, we'd think they were postcards from a museum. Her first husband and the love of her life, Heinrich Voll, died in an operation on his appendix and left her alone with their daughter. It was 1924, not a good time to be a single mother, but thanks to her looks she was able to marry again, this time to Papa Schneider.

And then his lovely wife was blown to bits and burnt up, and what was left of her lived on in a nightmare of wartime surgery. She was patched together out of strips of skin and buttered with codliver oil because the doctor had hit on the crazy idea that it nourished the healing process and that it was good for the skin not to dry out. It was torture, and Grandmother walked the banks of the Elbe wanting only to drown herself, screaming and screaming with the pain, *'Mein Gott, warum läßt du mich nicht sterben?'* She couldn't understand why she wasn't allowed to die and twice tried to commit suicide and rid herself of the bits of herself that remained, but they were not that easy to do away with, and in the end she hung a veil over her face, took the pain and the shame upon herself and went on living, a thing destroyed.

I never questioned what Grandmother looked like because I did not compare her with other grandmothers. On the contrary I compared them with her – and thought how strange they looked with their big ears and their big noses. When Mother and Father took me to museums, or when we were on a class outing to the Glyptotek Museum of Art, I walked round seeing Grandmother standing on every pedestal – minus nose and ears, minus hands and legs. For me she was classical beauty, and her face, like those of the statues, had stiffened into a lipless smile.

Tears came easily to Grandmother. She wept when we visited her, and she wept and waved her handkerchief when we drove off in the car. And every time she was touched by something – by some occasion, a sentimental film – she would weep and tell us how moved she was. *'Ich bin so gerührt,'* she would say. In the summer we would sit outside in the garden, and I would read aloud from Eichendorff, from Keyserling, or from Robert Walser – romantic books. *'Ach, wie schön!'* she would say when the story was over, tears rolling down her cheeks. I adored my grandmother, felt an infinite tenderness for her, and I would have plucked the stars out of the night sky for her if I could – and one day that's just what I did.

When I cycled the fifteen kilometres out to the bogs in Hannenov Wood, darkness was already beginning to thicken between the trees. The water was inky black and full of terrors. And then suddenly I could see them in the undergrowth. Glow worms! I took them home with me and, when everything was ready, I told Grandmother to come to the window and look out into the garden. The glow worms shone in the darkness, glinting on the lawn like stars and creating a constellation. Orion. We stood there for a long time, looking at it, until the glow worms crept away, and slowly the star formation began to fall apart, growing fainter, disappearing. I looked up at grandmother and waited in anticipation. There was nothing better than to hear her say it. *'Ich bin so gerührt!'*

As for my father's father, Grandfather, it was just like him to open up a bus route in a town that was too small and at a time when nobody had any money. It was not long before the novelty wore off and the bus ran empty. He moved the bus stops and put up more signs, changed the timetables and reduced the ticket price, but it made no difference. Things went steadily downhill, and morning after morning Grandfather got up to the humiliation of putting his cap on, sliding behind the wheel of the bus and driving round and round the town without a single passenger.

Grandfather was not one to give up easily and instead of learning his lesson would double the stakes. There could be no question of folding up the company. Quite the contrary. Now was the time for action. He increased his fleet and extended the timetable – and the route was no longer much too short but too long, and worst of all its destination was a place where no one wanted to go – Marielyst.

Marielyst was my grandfather's Las Vegas, and he was the only person who believed that this was the new Skagen, a Mecca for holiday-makers and health-seekers. Visitors would flock from Copenhagen, from Germany, and they would all need transporting. Just wait! It was nothing but bankrupted farmsteads, fields of sandy soil and wind-blown sea-walls with a solitary bathing jetty by the guesthouse, which stood empty for most of the year, and when Grandfather opened his grand bus route it led to nowhere.

'They'll be coming today,' he would say, letting out the clutch and driving off towards Marielyst. And when he returned in the evening without having sold a single ticket, he would say, 'Tomorrow.' Over supper he would talk himself to a pitch and babble about the beauties of nature, about woods of gold and green, and about holiday-makers all poised to flood this seaside resort from abroad, while today became this year and tomorrow next year and the one after, and the less food there was on the table the more he talked.

Once in a while there were brighter moments. Grandfather could see people standing at the bus stop on the main road and he would step on the accelerator, but when he got there it turned out to be nothing after all. His heart sank the first time he opened the door and tipped his cap with a 'Single or return?' – and they laughed and handed him some crates full of chickens and said, 'Single.' And so in the villages and farms along the route – especially for the children – standing at the roadside to make the bus stop developed into a cheap laugh. They were never going anywhere.

In the end Grandfather no longer stopped for them but drove out and back, motivated by routine and by the need to have something to do, and in the evenings he would still sit at the table and spout a bit about the growing cult of the great outdoors and about the hordes of tourists over the horizon, but he scarcely believed in it himself anymore and had reached the end of the road. He could not keep the creditors at bay and feed the family – they had nothing to live on – so one morning he said what everyone had been saying all the time, 'They're not coming,' and took the bus on its last trip.

He drove out along the main road towards Gedser and through Væggerløse and past the station, where a young man was standing at the bus stop. It had happened so often before. Grandfather did not stop. Why should he? But this time it was different. The man ran after the bus, shouting and waving his hat. He wanted to get on! Grandfather opened the door, and he climbed aboard and said *'Guten Tag'* and bought a single ticket and got off at the guesthouse.

'Marielyst Osterseebad,' Grandfather said in German and wished him a good stay – *'einen guten Aufenthalt.'* He had practised for years and now, when he needed it, it was, of course, too late.

Grandfather did not know whether to laugh or cry, and he looked out at the dikes with their lyme grasses, the white sand and the green stripes of water and the blue sky. He saw the beach populated with thousands of tourists, swimming and playing in the sand, and the Baltic overflowed in his eyes. Then he turned the bus around, drove back and dropped it off in town – and that was that. He went down and sat on the bench outside the station and there he remained, following the trains that trundled through, taking his life with them. It was the summer of 1914, and Carl Christian Johannes had given up.

The island of Falster actually lay below the surface of the sea and existed in people's consciousness only because they refused to believe otherwise. But, when they couldn't stand upright anymore, when they lay down to sleep, the water rose bit by bit and flowed in over the seawalls, over fields and woods and towns, and claimed the land back for the Baltic. I kept myself awake and saw it coming, looking out of the window at the black expanse of water filling the garden – the fish swimming round between the houses and the trees – and far away the town of Nykøbing sailing through the night like an ocean liner. The sky was full of starfish and I counted myself to sleep. In the morning the tide ebbed, and the water slipped away, retreating as people woke in their beds and got up to spend yet another day persuading each other that they existed and that Falster existed and that it all had a place on the map. The town smelt of sea and fish – the streets were full of seaweed and stranded jellyfish – and sometimes I found a conch or a fossilized sea urchin and put them in the drawer with the rest of my evidence of Atlantis.

There was a hole in our house where you could listen and music and voices would come out. This was the transistor radio. It stood in the kitchen and was caked in cooking fat, its aerial held together with tape, and my mother listened to it all day long when Father was at the office. Apart from me it was her only company, and she washed up to the sounds of 'Record requests', cooked to 'Karlsen's quarter-hour', polished the silver to 'That was the day that was' and vacuumed to the sound of the midday concert, a cheroot in her mouth and a glass of vodka at hand. They played Beethoven and Brahms and Tchaikovsky to the accompaniment of a hoover, which ran up and down the music with a rhythmic drone, making long phrases in the hallway and short and powerful thrusts in the dining room where the carpet needed an extra going over. When all was quiet and clean, I was sent to the garage with the hoover bag, and it all got chucked into the dustbin with the rubbish – the music, the coughs, the voices, the applause. I lifted the lid and peered in – a couple of bars of the Pastoral Symphony leaked out, smelling of mould and fermented apples. I slammed it shut, and not a note was left. My father did not care for music.

Occasionally it got really cold in winter, and then I knew that Germany was calling. We would soon be going down to visit my mother's stepsister, Aunt Eva, and her husband, Uncle Helmut, and their three sons, Axel, Rainer and Claus. Mother and Father packed the car full of warm clothes and suitcases and presents, and I hopped onto the backseat behind Mother, who had made sandwiches for the journey. Father would double-check the front door, close the garden gate and peer into the boot one last time to make sure everything was packed as it should be. He squeezed himself behind the wheel with hat and gloves on – his legs were too long for him to sit normally – adjusted the rearview mirror and read off the petrol gauge and the mileage which was exactly 9874.5, he said, noting the number and the time in his diary. We were two minutes behind schedule for the ferry. 'Passport, money, papers,' we said in unison, and then Father turned the key in the ignition, Mother lit a cheroot and turned up the traffic report on the radio, and we were off down Hans Ditlevsensgade, rounding the corner and journeying far back in time.

We stiffened when the officer checked us at the border, each becoming the spitting image of the photo in our passport – and for an instant we were smiling in black and white. Then it was over, and the motorway lay ahead. Mother unscrewed the duty-free and drank from the cap. We laughed and sang – and father asked her to turn the radio down and go easy on the vodka. That's enough now! Twenty years before she had left Germany behind for the sake of my father, and she sat clutching her memories, looking out at the houses, the fields, the streets rushing past, and everything responded to her look, gleaming and glinting back at her. Softly under her breath she read out the names of towns on the road signs we passed and with her forefinger traced in Michelin the route that led home – Hamburg, Hannover, Göttingen, Frankfurt am Main – and it ran like a tear down the road map and came to rest in Oberfranken.

More and more fir trees appeared along the motorway, the hills became higher and turned into mountains, and when we turned off and took the final, dark stretch of main road to arrive in Münchberg the snow would be falling in heavy, white flakes. Mother shook me, whispering *'Wir sind da,'* and I woke up among hundreds of miles of sweet papers, peered out through the window and wiped away the mist with my sleeve. We drove through the arched gateway, and the headlights lit up the drive to the large house. It stood at the top of a hill looking like a castle with its towers and parkland and ancient trees, and here they lived surrounded by a winter landscape – the Hagenmüller family.

Aunt Eva and Uncle Helmut would be walking down the main stairway, waving to us, the sons standing stiffly in line with their short, blond hair and pressed trousers, bowing and greeting and shaking hands as though they were clockwork.

'Grüß Gott, Tante Hilde! Grüß Gott, Onkel Knut! Grüß dich, Vetter Knüdchen!'

Aunt Eva planted a sharp kiss on my cheek.

'Na, kleiner Knut, fröhliche Weihnachten,' she would say, her voice snapping her 'Happy Christmas' into piercing little splinters. She greeted Father and turned at last to Mother, stepping back to get a good look at her 'little mouse'.

'Schau mal einer an, das Hildemäuschen!'

'*Ach, Evamäuschen!*' exclaimed Mother – and they fell into each other's arms and hated each other beyond all saying.

The only one I liked was Uncle Helmut, who was small and round and bent because of the pains in his back. He had green eyes and wore glasses – and I felt as though he could see right through me and was surveying my bone structure and my inner organs when he pinched my cheeks and prodded my stomach to get me to laugh to order, like a doctor getting you to say 'Aaaah'. I laughed and laughed and could already feel a cold coming on, and Uncle Helmut listened to it, thought long and hard and then pronounced his diagnosis and popped me a sweet from his pocket. It tasted of camphor, and that was good for most things, he said, and we went in together.

Uncle Helmut was a radiologist and spent his days taking pictures of people and telling them whether they would live or die. He came home for lunch and drank a glass of snaps before going back and taking some more photographs. The whole town filtered through his clinic. Strangers and acquaintances, friends and family – sooner or later their turn would come. It was taking its toll on him, and he grew paler and paler from the flash that showed things in their true light, felt more and more pain in his back, coughing and collapsing little by little. After work and dinner were over, he withdrew in silence, trudging up the stairs with a bottle of wine and locking the door to his room in the attic to continue what were called his 'studies'. No one knew what they were, these secret sciences.

Uncle Helmut believed in spirits and had good reason

to. As a seventeen-year-old he had been sent to the Eastern Front and had marched on Stalingrad. Two millions deaths later he marched back through the Russian winter, losing three toes and his sanity. He saw his parents standing beyond the grave, shielding him from enemy fire and frost, and even though he made it back alive, he never really returned home. He lived in the past with his family, surrounded by ghosts that only he could see, and the hallucination of life before the war was all that remained to him once it was over.

Over the years Uncle Helmut collected ancestral heirlooms and antiques, any item he could get his hands on that had been in the family, and he placed them in corners and on chests of drawers and hung them on walls, turning the house into a mausoleum for the family. It was full of relics from grandparents, great-grandparents, great-great-grandparents – all the way back to the armour that stood at the top of the stairs and rattled round the house at night as Uncle Helmut sleepwalked, marching on through that eternal winter. For their confirmations he gave his sons signet rings that belonged to the family and placed them between portraits and armour and family silver, and there they stood with no hope of escape, for their fate was sealed with the coat of arms and red wax.

I was envious of them and felt myself cheated of my part of the story, and on one of those days before Christmas Uncle Helmut told me to come up to his room after dinner and I would get something that was better than a ring, and he winked at me. The minutes crawled at a snail's pace, and I thought the meal would never end. The dessert dragged on and melted on our plates, before he said *'Mahlzeit,'* laid his serviette to one side, pushed back his chair and rose from the table. He took his wine, went up the stairs to his room and closed the door. I was already standing outside, and the knocking on the panelled door was the beating of my heart. I've had it now, I thought, as Uncle Helmut opened the door and wished me good evening.

It was a welter of books and papers, and shelves lined every wall. He began to tell me about the things in the room – a Samurai sword he had brought home from Japan, Indian prayer bells, the antlers on the wall. He sat down behind the desk, which was covered in parish registers and old photographs. This was where he sat at night, studying and drawing family trees that grew ever more fantastic branches as he drank his way through the bottle. A wreath hung behind glass in a frame above the desk, bound together by a black bow, and he explained that it was a plait that had been cut from his grandmother's hair when she died in 1894. It had hung in his parents' sitting room in memory of her. Uncle Helmut coughed and fell silent, looking me straight in the eye so I knew that now it was coming, and he opened the drawer.

There was no such thing as withdrawal in the German Army, he said – and placed a small piece of metal on the desk. Uncle Helmut showed me the scar on the underside of his arm and told me about the battle that had been the cause of it and about their retreat through Russia. When they needed supplies, they had to send advanced troops out to beat back the SS, who were defending the depots against their own soldiers. They managed to hold their position for as long as it took the company to run past and to have food, clothes and ammunition shoved into their hands, and then they continued westwards, fleeing annihilation. Uncle Helmut sighed, rolled his sleeve down and handed me the piece of metal. It was a piece of a Russian hand grenade, and now it was mine.

Uncle Helmut was full of fragments of grenade, which came out of his body at regular intervals, and every time we met he gave me a new piece and told me more about the war, until fragment by fragment I pieced the stories together. They were about survival but always ended with a corpse, and the only thing he could do was to drag it out for as long as he could. Sometimes he would come to a standstill, losing himself in the details of a landscape or describing a uniform jacket and counting all the buttons. When I asked who it had belonged to, he answered that the man had been lost in action and gave me the fragment – and there would be no more stories until next time.

Apart from me there was no one who thought much of Uncle Helmut really. Or rather, my mother was fond of him, and I suppose my father was too, but his wife and children weren't. The strongest feeling they had for him was fear, and an oppressive cloud hung over the house. Aunt Eva had married him for his money and because he was one of the few men left to marry after the war, while the sons crept around like dogs with their tails between their legs and agreed with everything he said. For them it was one big act. When they smirked and went about their duties, when they sat and ate nicely at table, I could see behind their movements the cogs turning round and was sure they were mechanical dolls wound up by fear – fear of beatings, of being confined to their room – and most of the time I kept myself to myself.

It came as a release when Christmas was over and we were to return home. I couldn't wait to get away from the ghosts in that icy house that gave you a cold the moment you walked through the door. Mother and Father packed the car and we said our thank you's and goodbye's and posed out on the terrace for the last time – it was snowing – and Uncle Helmut waved his hand and asked us to bunch up – Aunt Eva, Axel, Rainer and Claus, Mother and Father and I. Then we said 'Cheese', and he raised the camera to his eye and pressed the button, and I screamed and screamed and screamed, but it was too late. The picture was taken, and I knew that Uncle Helmut would be able to see from it which of us would die.

Every time we had to go out shopping it was the same old story. Mother sighed, fished out the shopping bag and put on her fur coat – it was yellow with black spots, an ocelot, and Father had said that it kept an eye on her. If anyone came too close – so I imagined – they would get eaten. Mother put on a matching fur hat, then she reached for my hand and gave me a melancholy smile.

'So, Knüdchen, jetzt gehen wir einkaufen,' she said, and we

summoned up our courage, took a deep breath and went
into town.

The baker was a few streets further down on Enighedsvej, and there was a moment's hush when we walked in
through the door and people stared at us and turned away.
We stood in a queue that grew longer and longer, and it was
never our turn. Mother might say 'Excuse me?' and maybe
raise a faint hand, but no one responded, and so it went on
until the girls behind the counter couldn't keep it up any
longer and sniggered, exchanging glances with the others in
the shop, and asked Mother what it was she wanted.

Mother asked for a white loaf and wholegrain rye bread
and a litre of milk and half a pound of butter. Her voice
was nervous, her accent thick, and they filled our bags with
sour milk, rancid butter and stale bread, and gave us too
little change, and Mother bowed her head, mispronouncing
her 'Thank you' and 'Sorry', and we hurried out and never
returned. We walked up Grønsundsvej and into butcher
Bengtsen on the corner and over the bridge to the greengrocer on Østergade and to Jeppesen's coffee shop on Slotsgade – and in shop after shop it was the same thing over
and over.

Mother and I made our daily rounds through a town
that had turned its back on us. We saw everything from
behind and all we met were people hurrying away from us
or waving a hand to ward us off when Mother approached.
They looked the other way. Doors were slammed shut,
goods were sold out, chairs were taken, and at Christmas
after church the priest withdrew his hand. We were the only

people in the world. Mother held my life in her hands as I held hers, tripping along at her side when the two of us went to the market square together and hurried all the way back home.

It was a relief to lock the door behind us and to be standing safely in our own hall. Mother hung the ocelot in the wardrobe and went up to the kitchen to put away the things we had bought. Then she would pour herself a glass of vodka, go down into the sitting room and put on a record. She would light a cheroot and lean back in the sofa breathing out smoke, and the rest of the afternoon she would spend partying by herself and listening to hits from the Germany of the '30s – Zarah Leander, Marlene Dietrich or Heinz Rühmann – and thinking about Berlin.

My mother was blonde and beautiful, and she had lived her life to the full before the Nazis came and took it. She arrived in Berlin to study in 1939 and lived in a classy place for young women called Victoria Studienanstalt. There were parks and porters and parlour maids, and the strict house rules were there only to be broken. She studied at the university by day and partied by night. They drank champagne, danced to American music and made fun of busts of Hitler by sticking ice-buckets on his head. Even though she sometimes sat for six or seven hours in the cellar when the air-raid sirens sounded, they carried on with their parties afterwards, she said, and didn't think about the war. It was way off in the distance, something you read about in the papers – and her friend, Inge Wolf, had taken her final exams even as the Russians were entering the city.

I could picture Mother waltzing through the smoking ruins of Berlin to the sounds of Zarah Leander singing *Davon geht die Welt nicht unter*, while Inge was up in front of the blackboard answering the examiners on that day of judgement, and none of it seemed that dangerous. Mother made light of it, telling me about the work camps where they had to do social service so they could go to university – it was called *Arbeitsdienst* – and where female camp commandants had their hair plaited in coils, wore brown dresses and were out-and-out sadists. At six o'clock there was *Fahnenappel*, the morning roll call, when the flag was raised – *Sieg Heil!* – followed by gymnastics before breakfast. They worked on the farms in blue overalls, hacking beets, emptying latrines and spreading their contents on cabbages as manure, and in the evenings they would be schooled in Nazism. After that, cabbage was served up and then it was bed. Mother played the accordion for community dancing and got up the nose of the camp commandants, who hated her for her beauty, her pride and her wealth. They sent her out to pick the caterpillars off the cabbages in the fields all day long, and at morning roll call it was, *'Hilde Voll, vortreten!'* And she would step forward and be given a dressing down. She was subversive by nature. She was inflaming the camp. *'Du hetzt das Lager auf!'* It was the same old story at every camp they were made to set up before the war – and so much the better, for the main thing was at all costs to avoid being sent to a munitions factory.

Mother put on a fresh record, *Das Fräulein Niemand*, humming along to the words.

Miss Nobody loves the Prince of Nowhere;
When he is near, so happy is she.
They both of them live in a castle of air
In the land of dreams by the Golden Sea.

Then she talked about her childhood friend, Stichling. His father had been chief of police in Kleinwanzleben, where she grew up, and he had a skeleton key, and they had let themselves in all sorts of places in the town, and Grandmother loved him. He had gone into the cavalry and become a tank commander. Mother fell silent. The record was finished, and that was the last I heard of him.

My mother was a woman of the world who had become stranded on the edge of the world, and she had lost more in Nykøbing, had let herself go more than I ever realised. After the war she left the remnants of her life behind – her family and her name, her country, her language – and moved to Denmark because she fell in love with Father. She put up with the humiliation, the contempt, allowed the hatred of Germans to fall on her head, and carried on loving Father and calling him her Apollo. He was her be-all and end-all, he was all she had – no one else would consort with a German. Mother sighed in that way of hers and said *'Ach ja'* and then took a puff of her cheroot and emptied her glass before putting on *The Threepenny Opera*, and we sang 'Mack the Knife' and 'Cannon Song' and 'Pirate Jenny', and when it came to the place where they ask her who is to die, we answered in unison, 'Everyone!'

I always hoped that it would be just as it was in the

song, that a ship would come with fifty cannons and bomb Nykøbing to smithereens and rescue us and take us far away. When I was down at the harbour playing, I would stand looking out for the ship, would imagine it sweeping up the sound with all sails set and laying anchor out there. Then the Jolly Roger would be run up the masthead and the bombardment would begin. And before the day was over the town would be pulverized to a heap of dust and rubble, and the day of vengeance would have come. A tribunal would be set up in the Market Square, and they would find out who my mother was, and the neighbours and the baker's shop-girls and the butcher and the greengrocer and the priest and the children and all the others would kneel with a single neck on the block. We would smile to each other, Mother and I, and then we would say *'Hopla!'* and the heads would roll on and on forever.

M y father's mother, Karen, we called Farmor, and she had a broad, serious face. She had lost her mother when she was twelve, and managing a girl and two half-grown boys as well as the farm ended up being too much for her father. He sent her off to live with her Auntie Bondo in Store Heddinge, and she grew up in her drapery shop, which was an offshoot of the Flensborg Department Store. Auntie Bondo was old and would forget that Karen was there at all. Most of the time she was left to her own devices and went around missing her father and her brothers, pining for her mother and having really no one at all. In the afternoons she would sit in the shop among the underwear, the dresses, the rolls of fabric, and wait for the right man to come and carry her off. She dreamt of romance wrapped in tulle, of passion in chiffon, of love eternal crocheted in lace, and she was sold the moment Carl showed up. He was tall and handsome and told her stories about Canada, promising to take her with him and planning it all in the minutest detail. And she crawled out from under the piles of tulle and chiffon and lace, said yes and gave him her first kiss.

It was the spring of 1902 when Farmor and Grandfather had got engaged. They then ran off to Copenhagen together without Auntie Bondo noticing – or maybe she just didn't care. They were married in the Garrison Church. Once his military service was over, Karen was pregnant, and they returned to Falster and leased Orehoved Hotel. It looked out across the Great Sound, and Grandfather's eyes could follow the tongue of water to Masned Island and, further out, to Zealand. He could see the railway ferry sailing in and he pinned his hopes on transport, having read in the papers that there was no stopping its growth. Trade and tourism were the future and would transport them off and away, right across the Atlantic!

Guests were few and far between at the start, but that was how it always was. It took time for a place to get a name. Grandfather spread the word as best he could and stuck signs with arrows on the roadside, while Karen looked after the child, cleaned and cooked and ran a hotel that had no guests. She changed sheets that had not been slept in, put fresh flowers in vases no one would see, and Grandfather placed advertisements in the papers and gave the hotel five stars. He described all its comforts and mod cons, pouring praise on a landscape that was flat and fog-bound, inventing attractions where there was nothing worth looking at, and every evening Karen took her place in reception and prepared to receive travellers who never came. The ferry docked, and the traffic drove past the hotel. No one had anything to stop for in Orehoved.

After a couple of seasons in an empty hotel their plans lost their romantic glow, and they decided that they would rely on local trade instead, on running an inn – dinners and parties, perhaps even music and dance to attract a wider clientele. That would do the trick! They'd have guests for lunch and a dish of the day and the week's menu and the wine of the month and seasonal seasonings, and Grandfather hired a dance band for the Saturday and hung posters up. When they got to the end of the week, the tables and chairs stood untouched, and Karen took the lunches, the dish of the day, the week's menu and the seasonal seasonings and poured them all on the compost heap, and Grandfather still stood in the doorway with a roll of tickets and the wine of the month. The band played, and the lamps twinkled far into the night. Not a soul turned up. He might as well close down.

Grandfather threw himself into one event after the other, sending out invitations for special evenings – talks and discussions, port wine tastings, piano and song recitals – and even though he sat debating with himself and applauding music for which he and Karen were the only audience, he continued to insist that if you don't succeed at first, you try and try again, that the losers were those who gave up. There was nothing wrong with the idea. It was the way it was put into practice. And he talked about getting a national politician to pay them a visit. Or what about a famous cabaret artist? He wrote letters and waited for the postman, and then wrote more letters, and when bedtime came he would reassure Karen, insisting that soon their luck would turn – and then one day it happened.

Grandfather came running in with a letter. It was from an agent in Copenhagen, and he could put them in touch with stars from the world of the theatre, of culture. A week later Grandfather had already arranged a meeting and was climbing aboard the train to Copenhagen. Karen and he had not been separated since his stint in the Army, and it seemed like an eternity before the front door was flung open again and Carl stepped in, beaming and waving his hat and shouting, 'We are saved!' He took out a couple of glasses and a bottle of the wine of the month and told her about his trip to Copenhagen, about the agent and about how everything would be different from now on. 'Moving pictures,' he whispered and lifted his glass. They would open a picture theatre! They clinked their glasses and drank, and Farmor could scarcely hold back her tears because it all was too much, and she knew that this time it would all go wrong.

For Carl there was not the shadow of a doubt. He had seen the light and he set up his projection room in the restaurant, arranged the chairs in rows and hung up a screen.

He spoke to the press, and on Tuesday 17th July 1909 a notice appeared in *The Lolland-Falster Times* to the effect that, on the recommendation of the parish council, permission had been given for the establishment of a picture-house and that at 8 o'clock the following Saturday Orehoved Inn would open its doors for a motion picture show. Drinks would be served, and the show would be followed by music and dance – Grandfather staked everything on one throw. And people came in droves. They flocked in from Vordingborg and Nørre Alslev, and the farmers came walking across the fields carrying their Sunday shoes in a bag. Even squire Wilhjelm arrived from Orenæs in a horse-drawn carriage and sat himself down in the front row next to members of the town council and the parish priest, and Grandfather bade them all welcome and turned out the ceiling lights and got the projector rolling.

The screen began to flicker. Dust danced in the cone of light, and shadows began moving across the screen. Ahhh! Oooh! They saw a fisherman bid farewell to his family on the quayside and sail off with two friends. They capsize in the storm and drown, and his dead body is washed up on the seashore. There is a funeral. His wife and children stand at the graveside in mourning – and the reel ran out. It was as silent as the grave in the room. Grandfather scarcely dared turn on the light, and the audience sat as though turned to stone, staring straight ahead. And then from the fifth row came a soft sound. Someone was weeping, and she was followed by another and yet another, breaking down and sobbing. The priest went across to offer comfort, to hold her hand. People got up, crossing the room to offer their condolences, and the squire and the town officials hurried away without Grandfather being able to do a thing about it or stop them to explain the misunderstanding. It was the end of Orehoved Hotel.

The next day the flags all flew at half-mast in the town. People wore black and spoke in low voices and were in mourning for the remainder of that week. There was a funeral on the Sunday, the bells tolled, and the coffins were lowered. Grandfather had long since given up trying to explain that it was only a film, and, when Karen and he returned from the churchyard and sat at the dining table and she told him that she was pregnant with their second child, he poured a glass of wine and replied that they would have to move very soon.

It wasn't the mayor who was in charge, nor was it the police or the director of the Bank of Industry and Commerce. It wasn't people at all. It was the rooks. They flew around us, and they would scream and hop down the streets, and sit in clutches on the rooftops keeping a beady eye on us. The rooks emptied the dustbins, stripped the slaughterhouse clean and gathered in throngs down by the harbour when the fishermen came in. In spring they would fly behind the sowing machines, pecking up the seeds as quickly as they were scattered, and in the autumn they ravaged the orchards, stripping them of fruit. There was not a tree or lamp post that wasn't occupied by rooks. They left no one in peace. They ate everything and, if you stood still for too long, they would come and peck at you, too.

They were the first thing I heard in the morning, long before I woke, and the last I heard when I went to bed. I lay listening to the rooks coming closer, flying over the house, their cries filling the air, and I had no defence. I tried to cling to my room, to my toys, to sing *Baa, baa, black sheep* … , but it was no good. I was almost indistinguishable from the dark, and the terror would well up inside me until I could hold it back no longer and it burst its banks and my greatest fear became real and the rooks swooped down and took me.

There was no one to understand why I used to scream when the moment came to say goodnight, and it turned into an endless battle. I dragged things out as long as I could and I did my best to explain, but all that came out of my mouth were hoarse noises. In the morning the rooks flew up, and my arms flailed and only stopped when my mother shook me awake, saying, *'Knüdchen! Aufwachen!'* I was ill, feverish. Mother and Father consulted Dr Spock to read up about children's illnesses but couldn't work out what the matter was and rang for the doctor. He arrived with a black bag – his name was Dr Kongstad – felt my forehead, looked down my throat and took my pulse. Then he said it was whooping cough, wrote a prescription, snapped his bag shut and left. And I swallowed the pills and was given apples and juice. I did what they expected, what was written on the label, and everyone agreed that I was getting better when the bottle was empty.

From then on I knew the best thing was to pretend that nothing was wrong. When I went to kindergarten with Miss Freuchen, I copied the others as well as I could, laughing when they laughed and playing along with their games. I bit a little, but wouldn't open my mouth when the others sang *There is a black bird and it's singing in the tree*, though that got better and disappeared once I started school. When I biked through West Wood on my way to football with the Lilliput team, it didn't bother me to hear them shrieking in the trees. I scrambled into my kit – blue jersey and stockings and white shorts – and acted normally, running around between the rooks across the tussocky field. You could follow the game from way off, watching the advantage pass from one side to the other as the ball made the birds fly up.

They hung out across in the wood where they had their nests – it was a real witches' coven in there with bird droppings hanging from the branches in long stalactites. This was also the site of 'Falster City Camping – An oasis in a city of opportunities'. There was an ice cream stall, and German tourists would sit in front of cottage tents and caravans, and despair. They had been seduced by the child-friendly beaches, the idyllic landscape, the snug little market town, all as described in the brochure. Of the colony of rooks not a word had been said.

They were woken from their dream holiday by the din that began at dawn, and towards evening the rooks would assemble in huge flocks out in the fields, fly in across the town and settle back in West Wood. Then came the worst of it all, when it would rain bird droppings. Shops put their wares under cover, washing was taken in, and people with open umbrellas and gumboots hurried through the muck. Most people stayed in, sitting and shaking their heads, listening to the droppings that drummed against window panes filthying everything. The tourists packed their bags and fled as far as they could go – and not a soul watched them go without wishing to join them. Night would have fallen before anyone dared take to the streets again, and life took up where it had left off, even though everyone knew it was on borrowed time. We were food for the birds. The rooks ruled the roost in Nykøbing.

I loved Grandmother's cooking. She made *Wienerschnitzel* and *Kalbsfleischgeschnetzeltes mit Rösti*, but best of all was her *Gullasch*. She would stand in the kitchen busily cooking among her old pots and her butcher's knives while the pork and the onions spat and sizzled in the pan. The air was full of spices – paprika and cinnamon and pepper – that made you sneeze, and the steam billowed up from the saucepans, filling the house with fragrances that nothing could match. It was hard not to stick a finger in to taste, and, when the moment finally arrived and the *Gullasch* was served, my world exploded on my palate into tastes that reached deeper and deeper and never had an end. It felt as though you had been far away on a distant journey, as though many years had passed, when you found yourself back in the sitting-room, your face glowing, and took yet another mouthful.

Grandmother's *Gullasch* was irresistible. Once tasted, it would make you want more, would have you licking your plate forever. It would only come to an end when Grandmother said stop and took the casserole and put it in the fridge with a tea towel over the lid. There it would remain, and I could think of nothing else and grew hungrier and hungrier. As soon as Mother was out of the house, as soon as she had gone into town with Grandmother, I would run to the kitchen and look at the casserole in the fridge. There was one helping left. Sticking my fingers into it told me that the *Gullasch* tasted better than ever and it transported me all the way back to my great-grandmother, who fried pork and onions in the casserole a hundred years ago – Lydia Matthes. She put in the paprika and tomato purée and garlic, the ginger and juniper and caraway – and when it was boiling hot, she poured in the red wine and the beef stock. Slowly my great-grandmother would brew her *Gullasch*, letting it simmer for hours, reducing it until the meat was tender. She would keep one helping to use as stock, and that was how the taste grew stronger and richer as the years went by, until Grandmother inherited the casserole, doing as she had done and making sure there was always a little bit left over for the next batch of *Gullasch*.

The casserole was black and heavy and made of cast iron, and it was almost lost at the end of the war. Grandmother and Papa Schneider had to flee Kleinwanzleben because the Russian troops were coming, and all they managed to do was to roll up their paintings, bury their wine and lock their doors. Then the English came and evacuated them. They drove off in lorries full of the sugar beet seeds that Papa Schneider propagated and that must not fall into the hands of the Communists. He wasn't able to take anything with him – except the reflex camera that he managed to smuggle under his coat. The casserole remained behind with its stock, and they would have lost that along with everything else if it hadn't been for Mother.

Mother had left Berlin in 1942 and had run off to Austria. They had not heard from her for a long time, and Grandmother was sick with worry, not knowing whether she was dead or alive. She hid herself well away from the war and the Nazis on a mountain in Steiermark, where she lived in a convent and ate potatoes, sticking it out for a winter, a summer and another winter, waiting for the war to be over and done with. During the final months of the war it became clear to her that the dividing line was going to be the Elbe and that Kleinwanzleben lay on the wrong side and would be occupied by the Russians. There wasn't a moment to lose! They had to get out. She tried to contact the family to warn them, but it was too late. All lines of communication were dead. She searched her heart, and decided to go to their rescue, to travel home.

She took the first available train from Graz. No one could say whether it would leave and certainly not whether it would arrive. Most of the railway network had collapsed, and what was left was under constant attack. The train set off and travelled for an hour or two. Then they felt it brake, and everyone jumped off and threw themselves face down on the siding. The planes dive-bombed them, strafing the train and dropping bombs, and once they had gone it was quickly up again and on, covering as many kilometres as they could before the next air attack. They travelled eastwards because that was where there were still railway tracks, but it was the wrong direction, towards Prague, so Mother got off and found a train heading for the most terrible destination on earth – Berlin. A week later she had crossed Hungary and Czechoslovakia and was stepping out of a carriage riddled with holes onto the platform at Anhalter Bahnhof. The only thought in her mind was how to get out of there and, running for her life, she took a wild chance and scrambled aboard the last train to make it out of the city just as Berlin was blown to kingdom come behind her.

It was a miracle that Mother got to Magdeburg alive. It was bang on the front line, with American troops on one side and German troops on the other, and the bombs were raining down on the town. There were five kilometres to Kleinwanzleben, and Mother was ready to drop with hunger and exhaustion. She stole a bicycle and rode along the main road through a thunderstorm of artillery fire, and there at the end of her strength stood the house on Breite Weg. She ran up the steps. The door was locked, and she hammered on the windows. No one came. It was empty. She crawled in through a cellar window and wandered round calling their names – it was clear that they had fled in haste – and Mother hoped for the best. Her legs were giving way under her and she sat down heavily in the kitchen. And then she remembered the *Gullasch*.

She opened the door to the pantry. The casserole stood where it had been abandoned a couple of days before. It had the fragrance of A Thousand and One Nights, of the Garden of Eden and temptation whispered, inviting you closer, leading your hand down to the spoon, the dream was already so tantalizingly close that you couldn't resist, could only follow your only desire, which was to eat – and Mother put the lid back on. If she gave in now and ate the rest, it would all be over, and the stock would be lost forever. With hunger raging inside her, she took the casserole under one arm, put it on the luggage rack and cycled out to the German army to find a safe haven and find her family and return the casserole to Grandmother.

This was how Grandmother could continue to serve a *Gullasch* that was a hundred years old, and it tasted sweeter and stronger with every secret spoonful I slipped down. I was so intent on eating that I never heard the door open, got a shock when Mother was suddenly standing in the kitchen screaming, *'Was tust du?!'* What had I done? She was staring with wild eyes at the spoon clenched in my hand – I had scraped the bottom so as to leave nothing behind – and only then did I realize what I had done. My horror and remorse knew no end, but there was no going back. What was done was done. I smiled an apology with *Gullasch* plastered across my face. I looked at my mother, looked at the spoon and then, praying for her forgiveness, opened my mouth for the final spoonful.

M y father shot up. He was tall and thin, and when I clambered up on his shoulders I could look across the hedge to the far horizon. He was too big to take in all at one go, so I knew him only in bits – he had a large nose and large ears and large feet. His boots, he would say, had been built in a boatyard. No matter where we were – in a restaurant, a cinema – he would complain about the lack of leg room, and we'd leave again. His arms reached to his hands, no further, and those hands were a long way off and kept the world at a distance. His forehead increased in height as his hair fell out – and Mother thought he was the handsomest man in the world.

Father was as kind as the day was long and his eyes warmed you like the sun. He didn't smoke, he didn't drink, he was early to bed and early to rise, and I never heard him utter a swearword. He was always on time, always conscientious in his work, always paid his taxes. And 100 metres before a traffic light he would slow down, so that, even if it was green, by the time we reached the junction it would be sure to have turned red. He stood up automatically if he was talking to someone in authority on the telephone and would never put a plug in a socket without first having read the instructions. He was correct through and through, from top to toe, his conscience as clean as his shirt, and his tie was tied, his shoes were polished and his suit so crisply pressed it could stand on its own two creases.

Father was an insurance man, and every day he made sure that nothing would happen. The alarm went off at half-past six. Father got up, drank his coffee, ate his breakfast roll, kissed Mother goodbye – and then drove to work along the same route he had taken for fifty years. He worked at Danish Building Assurance in the town square, and his first question when he came through the door was 'Has anything happened?' Nothing had, and Father heaved a sigh of relief, went into his office and got on with insuring everything there was to insure on Falster. He dealt with the church and the town hall, with man and beast, while houses, cars and bicycles were all covered for theft and fire and water and rot and storm and any accident that could conceivably strike the planet. Father always assumed the worst would happen, pre-empting damage, wrestling with the unforeseeable and finding no peace until everything was safely secured. He sighed with satisfaction when he opened *The Falster Times* in the morning, and there was nothing in it. The paper could just as well have been blank. Nothing happened, nothing whatsoever. The days repeated themselves without even a leaf falling to earth, and surely and steadily life ground to a halt.

It was a task that could have no end. Father bore the world on his shoulders – there was always something or other to worry about – and his moods rose and fell with the barometer that hung on the wall in the living room. Arranging his face into earnest furrows, he would tap the glass. When the needle showed fair, his face lit up, but it wouldn't be long before he was tapping again and thinking about low pressure and rain and lightning strikes. He spoke of the October storm in 1967 as though it was an episode from the Bible. Summer brought the danger of fire – he hoped it would be wet – and winter awoke anxiety about frost damage and snow, and he never wanted a white Christmas. 'Shhh!' he would say and hold his breath, his forefinger pointing heavenwards, when we got to the most important bit of the news – the weather forecast.

Father came home for lunch on the dot of half-past twelve and sat down to a hot meal, and in the evening I would hear the car drive up Hans Ditlevsensgade and come to a halt in the garage. Then the front door would open and close, and Father would call 'Hello there!' and hang up his hat and coat in the wardrobe. We would hurry up into the kitchen, where Mother would be beaming and saying *'Ach, Väterchen!'* and kissing him on the cheek and loving him beyond all saying. We laid the table in the dining room, where everything had its allotted place and stood on the table in systematic order – the porcelain, the napkins, the salt and pepper, the vases full of flowers – and Father had eyes in the back of his head. When I opened a drawer in the sideboard to take out the knives and forks, he was on to it in a flash.

'What do you want?' he'd ask, and then he would shake his head and tell you what to do and how. 'The forks are in the top middle drawer. No, not there, the middle, at the back.' And so it would go on. Father pursued his insurance business at home and went into the minutest detail. It was impossible to do anything right – and he would forever be adjusting the grandfather clock even though it kept perfect time.

To move was in itself to challenge providence. 'Careful!' he would say before you had even taken a step, and if you asked him for something – never mind what – he would say no. For him there was nothing worse than a draught. 'Shut the door!' he would shout as you opened it, and, when you closed it behind you, he would ask you to do it again – and do it properly. Father always thought there was something not quite shut. 'There's a draught,' he would say and would walk around testing the air, checking the windows, drawing the curtains, until every last hole was plugged and all movement ceased. The floorboards creaked, the doors groaned, the walls had ears, and I was silent and careful and did as he said. I longed for the day when he would stop it and just let things be, but that day never came.

There was no chink in the iron control that Father exerted over his surroundings. If he so much as glanced away, everything would disappear, never to be found again. All he ever did was to keep checking, reassuring himself that reality really did exist, that everything was in place and happened at the right time. When he spoke, it was to state accepted truths – 'They say … ', 'What people do is … ' – and all he expressed were self-evident truths. For him all talk was in one sense a telling, a kind of counting, and when he wanted to recount something it turned into a catalogue of prices and shopping lists, inventories of our possessions – the centrepieces, the bronze clock, the carpets – balanced against what they had cost. And that was a long story. In the most literal sense what he did was register life. For him it consisted of facts and figures, and he would observe that it was cloudy, or that it was late – that was just how things were. Afterwards he would sit and write it all down in his Mayland diary, duration and location, income and expenditure, price of petrol, mileage, time and temperature. He counted the days and added them together, smiling each time they added up to a year he could draw a line under, and the diaries were set side by side on a shelf, where they provided accounts of every year from 1950 onwards.

Father watched over us twenty-four hours a day and 365 days a year. It felt as though our lives would collapse about our ears if he relaxed for one moment. After dinner he would begin all over again, brushing the crumbs off the tablecloth and putting the cutlery back in the sideboard. He counted the knives, the forks, the spoons and locked the drawer. Then he took the key, returning it to the bureau and locking that too. He ranged things in order, put things away, turned off anything that was lit, pulled plugs out of sockets to prevent short circuits, and placed the silver candlesticks in the washing basket – just in case. He checked the radiators, which had to be set at 2½ precisely, went out and closed the garage doors and the garden gate before locking the doors to the house – the front door, the garden door, the cellar door and the doors to the utility room and the garage – and then he hid the keys to make sure no one could break in. Once he had finished locking up and checking lights and packing the house away for the night, he would kiss Mother and me goodnight and lie down in bed. Then he took the key of keys and placed it in his pyjama pocket, drew the duvet over him and, with a mind at ease in the knowledge that all was secure, he would click the lamp on the bedside table, and the last light in the universe went out.

F or some reason or another, I decided on ham sand-wiches, and that was what I took with me to school. I wouldn't have anything else. There was something wrong – I could feel it quite clearly – and they began to talk behind my back and laugh at me and move away from my table when we had our dinner break. I didn't know why and did my best to fit in, but it got worse and worse, until finally there was someone who pointed a finger and said it to my face. It was my ham sandwich. Instead of being cut lengthways with crust around each slice, it was cut across with the crust on the ends – and that was not how you did it in Denmark.

Mother sliced bread the way she was used to doing in Germany, and I could not bring myself to tell her. I went to school with my alien ham sandwich and chewed my way through the lunch break, but after a while I stopped taking it out of my school bag at all. I left it there, tried to pretend all was as it should be and after school I cycled round trying to find a place where I could throw my packed lunch away without being noticed.

This wasn't as easy as I had thought. There were either too many people or too few, and I was sure that someone would see me through the window if I threw it into a garden. There was always something that held me back, and at last I chucked the package of sandwiches in between some bushes and cycled on. But I knew straightaway that my mother would walk past that very spot and find it, so I turned around, fished it out and took it home with me.

Even before I got past the garage it was more than I could bear. I parked my bike and ran up the cellar steps shouting 'Hiya!' to Mother. She was standing in the kitchen, and I looked at her, my face wreathed in smiles for fear of discovery. My guilty conscience was smouldering in my school bag. I went to my room and carefully opened the drawer of my desk – it was the only place that I could call my own and that could be locked. I held my breath, laid the packed lunch in the drawer, closed it as quickly as I could when I heard my mother calling from the living room, *'Knüdchen! Händewaschen! Essen!'* and obediently went to wash my hands before eating.

My mother would sit at the table with her cheroot and a beer while I ate. She looked knotted and tense and almost always sad. The only thing holding her in place was her will, and she locked herself inside herself and clenched her fists until they looked like hand grenades, the knuckles shining white. I would have given my life to make her happy, would often take one of her hands and stroke it and tell her about my day. We had played football, and I had gone up to the blackboard. Susanne had got braces and the twins were sending out invitations to their birthday … And it was all lies. For the day had been spent being a German pig, hiding in the breaks, hiding my packed lunch, my bike, my clothes. For everything I had they poured scorn on, even on her name, jeering and sneering, 'Hildegard! Hildegard!' You couldn't be called that! I was never able to bring myself to tell Mother and diverted her as best I could. And she would look at me and slowly open her hand, and into its palm I placed what I had and hoped that it was enough.

Mother was alone in a foreign country and as lonely as a body can be. Ever since she was little, all she had known was the loss of those she loved, one by one, and nothing – not even the vodka bottle in the kitchen cupboard – could console her. Her father, Heinrich Voll, was taken to hospital with appendicitis in 1924 and died on the operating table. He was an eye specialist, a gentle, happy man, and between him and Grandmother had been a marriage of true love. Their photograph stood in a silver frame in the living room at home, and showed them sitting on a slope looking across the valley, Grandmother beautiful, Heinrich in uniform. When the First World War broke out, he served as a medical officer and, when he was on leave from the front, he told her about the fox cub he had found in the woods and cared for, about how it had got well again, how he had set it free. After the war he opened a private practice in Halle an der Saale, and Mother would run round the place, playing in the apartment they had next door and popping in when he didn't have any patients. They would laugh together. Those were happy days – and in the twinkling of an eye her heart was wrenched from her. Her father was dead, she was six years old, and there was no greater misery on earth.

They stayed in the apartment, Grandmother and she, and would have had nothing to live off had it not been for the pension the doctors allotted them – 300 Deutschmarks a month – perhaps to salve their guilty consciences for the operation that had gone wrong. But inflation swallowed most of it up, the money became worthless, and, even though Grandmother rented out the practice and later more and more rooms in the house, things could only go from bad to worse. When at last they found themselves crammed into the smallest room that was left and could see no other way out, Grandmother took off her ring and surrendered to Papa Schneider, who had proposed to her. And one day she came home in tears and told Mother that she was being sent away for a time to live with his cousin in Biebrich.

Aunt Gustchen lived with her son and his wife and their two daughters in a little town on the outskirts of Wiesbaden. They were sectarian Protestants and belonged to 'The Church of the Confession', and there were only two things that interested them – the gossip from the parish council and their eternal war against Catholics and the archbishop in Mainz. Despite the fact that they owned vineyards by the Rhine, they didn't drink and would never even taste the wine. When we visited them once a year, it was just like stepping into an undertaker's.

Her son was a giant. Stooped and bowed under a weight of faith, he sat in the low-ceilinged room with his stick-like wife. Their daughters wore flounced dresses and now and then peeked sideways out of the corners of their eyes, their glances fluttering like sparrows pecking crumbs off the tablecloth. We would sit down round the table for coffee and fold our hands into steeples and say grace in time to the ticking of the clock.

Vater, segne diese Speise.
Uns zur Kraft und Dir zum Preise!

'Father, bless this food we eat. It brings us strength, Thy praises meet.' The house was riddled by Pietist madness. It sinuated itself in ivy and evergreens, Jesus hung on the wall weeping, and there were crucifixes everywhere and needlepoint in frames cross-stitched with Bible quotes in Gothic letters. Father would be fidgeting in his chair, trying to make room for his legs and doing his best to fit in, and I would look across at Mother and think of all she had gone through – and whisper 'Satan' instead of 'Amen'.

It was a chilly and sombre and joyless place. It was hard to imagine what it must have been like to lose your father and say goodbye to your mother and arrive here with a suitcase in 1926. Aunt Gustchen had a bun at the nape of her neck and a hairnet, wore buttoned black dresses and had never been young. Her mother had been a church warden's daughter from Thüringen and had been possessed by the devil – she was an epileptic – and Gustchen learned the fear of God at her mother's knee. She lived her life on the lip of the grave with her hands folded and a cross round her neck. They ate stale bread, scrimped and saved, never throwing anything away, despite being comfortably well-to-do, because wastefulness was a sin. She pounced upon the least sign of enjoyment and hounded the slightest pleasure – it was cheap to dress up and sinful to smile, while laughter was evil itself breaking the face into devilish grimaces.

Mother was sent to Sunday school and infected with lice. Her long fair hair was chopped off and her clothes were exchanged for an ugly black shift that rasped against her skin. She was given a prayer book, and they were always praying, following the church calendar on their knees. A year of birth, death and resurrection passed. And then another. And Mother kept waiting to hear from Grandmother and couldn't understand why she had not long since sent for her. She was sure that letters were not being passed on to her but were hidden away somewhere, and she dreamed of escape and cried herself to sleep so as not to wake Aunt Gustchen, who lay beside her in the bed, snoring with eyes wide open.

Mother had felt that she had been forgotten by the whole world, so when at last the message came it was as if a coffin lid had been lifted to let the sun stream in. She was to go to Kleinwanzleben and rejoin her mother and live with her stepfather! She had never met Papa Schneider, and now she took her suitcase and set off by train, thrusting her head out of the window to relish air and speed, and rushed to meet her mother at 100 kilometres an hour. At the station she was met by a servant girl, and together they walked through the streets and out along the country road until they reached the manor. It was surrounded by fields and had long red barns on either side and black timber framing and towers with steep roofs, and on the largest of these there was a clock. They crossed the courtyard and rang the bell. Papa Schneider opened the door, and Mother summoned up her courage, gave him the broadest smile she could muster, reached out her hand to this complete stranger whom she was about to make her father and said, *'Guten Tag, Vati.'*

In 1910 Grandfather and Farmor moved from Orehoved Hotel to one of the smartest addresses in Nykøbing. The name 'Bellevue' stood out in gold letters, and the house had three storeys with a look-out tower at the top built in green timber and clad in copper. Farmor could have fainted when Carl took out the keys and let himself in. The living rooms they walked through went on forever and their ceilings touched the sky. All Karen wanted was to get out as quickly as she could, but Grandfather told her not to worry. He was planning to open a haulage company and that would pay for the house and the children and more besides! It was just a question of speeding up developments, and then just wait and see! Before long the link between Copenhagen and Berlin would go straight as the crow flies, and Nykøbing bang in the right place, the new centre for business and tourism. And Karen never said a word but unpacked and hung the kitchen clock on the wall. A few years later he was bankrupt.

They were up to their ears in debt, and Grandfather at his lowest ebb sat on the bench down by the station watching the trains go past, staring at the world as he walked around, silent, refusing to talk to anyone. He kept himself to himself in the study at home, twiddling his thumbs in the dark behind drawn curtains, while his beard, his hair, his nails grew longer and longer and he gave up washing and eating. This carried on until Grandfather hit rock bottom and was dead to the world. Then he picked himself up, dusted himself down and started out afresh. There were endless opportunities! Nothing was impossible!

After the buses it was a shoe shop in Frisegade. It went bust. Parisian fashions were not made for hoeing beet, and people stood outside and laughed at the models in the shop window. Customers were so few and far between that when the shop bell jangled he jumped and asked people what they were doing there. Then he read about the Copenhagen Telephone Company in the paper – more than 50,000 subscribers – and tried to sell telephones to people who didn't know anyone but those who lived next door, and was left with hundreds of sets and no one to call. He sat himself down on the bench and shut himself away in his own world, but it wasn't long before he flung open the door again and was trying it out with motorbikes – Nimbus motorbikes! – and the cameras flashed and Grandfather was there, his arms spread wide, smiling to the press, who were on the spot photographing him with flags and spirits flying high in front of the next doomed enterprise.

His downfall could be followed year by year in *The Lolland-Falster Times*, and, as time went on and any hope of making things work out in reality fell apart, Grandfather began to invent. He bought on tick and kept creditors at bay with stories, coming up with one excuse after the other, and the worse things got the better the stories. Returns on shares in Canada! An equity advance from a distant uncle, guarantors whose signatures must have got lost in the post – he had just had a meeting with the barrister, who would contact them in person within the next few days! Grandfather was convincing, and he managed to swim abreast of the catastrophe as he gambled on a future that had to reach Nykøbing sooner or later, even though the town lay at the furthest corner of the earth – and he closed his eyes and begged the powers that be for it to be his turn before it was too late.

It was left to Karen to deal with everyday life and keep things ticking over. She had two children to look after, and then three, four – Leif and my father, Ib and their little sister Annelise – and she worked herself to the bone to put food on the table and clothes on their backs. She took on cleaning jobs on the side, did piecework in the strawberry fields in the summer, baked bread, grew vegetables and rechristened the soup every evening – onion soup, potato soup, consommé with egg – Grandfather asked if there was brandy in it, and there was – and she made it last so long that in the end it tasted of nothing but goodwill and pure love. She cut a heel out here, a toe out there and knitted and sewed and made the best out of nothing, while the things they did have were sold one by one, and when she came to the end of her day, she put the children to bed and bade them goodnight with a kiss and a small white lie.

They lived on air, and no one realised how bad things were – except Father. He grew taller and thinner, feeling the pinch as clothes and shoes didn't fit, and at Christmas knew that the presents were empty words packed in wrapping paper. He did what he could to help out at home, got good marks at school and when he turned fifteen left school and got a job as a trainee at the bank. He looked after Leif, who had spinal TB and limped in and out of hospital, covered Annelise's dancing lessons and paid the school money for his little brother Ib, who was into skiving and stealing and smoking. If anyone teased Leif for being an invalid, Father told them off and threatened to go to the police, after which they got stick from Ib, who hit them too hard and too long, his behaviour turning more and more criminal. Annelise used make-up and began going out on the town, and Father would fetch her home at night from the inn, the *Friser*. He got up in the morning and helped Ib with his homework, even though he hung out with the wrong crowd down at the quarry and was drinking. And after work Father would tuck a file under his arm and go to evening classes to learn bookkeeping and stenography and German, and when he put up his hand he had the correct answers at his fingertips.

The day he got the job at Danish Building Assurance – that day in 1934 – was the happiest of my father's life, and he needed no excuse to tell the story over and over again, remembering the advertisement in the newspaper and Director Damgård who received the applicants in the company's premises in the Market Square. He was a large man and had started the business from nothing with three employees, Frøken Slot, Max Christensen, who kept the books, and his son-in-law, Henry Mayland. Clients were reinsured and they saved two Danish crowns if they took out a ten-year policy – that kind of thing would be completely impossible nowadays! I heard Father tell the story at least a thousand times, and he always beamed when he came to the point when Director Damgård looked in at the office – it was late in the evening and he was working late – and asked him what he thought about bridge. Father had learned bridge from the old ladies in town – he was fond of visiting them, chatting to them – and he stepped into the breach as a fourth and played cards with the board and drank coffee and cognac and said no thanks to a cigar – and was promoted to chief clerk. Damgård had always thought highly of him, said Father, smiling at the thought, and then started the story all over again, retelling it like a gospel that spread light in a time of darkness.

There was a financial crisis, and there was no work to be had. Leif was sent to a sanatorium in Jutland, and the bills poured in. Ib was expelled from school and blew it every time he got a new apprenticeship. He swaggered around wearing a hat and flared trousers and somehow managed to be better off than Father. Even though it meant taking a chance – not something he was keen on – he got Ib employed as a trainee at Danish Building Assurance in order to keep an eye on him. It went well at first, and then it started going too well to be true. Ib charmed and fast-talked his way, making more promises than he could keep. They got more customers than ever, but it was one big fiddle. He had his hand in the till and was eating out and playing the fat cat, buying drinks all round. It was a scandal, and it was left to Father to smooth things out, to apologise to the board and to Director Damgård – he would make sure everything was put right – and he settled the accounts and brought the clients back into the fold. Then he got hold of Ib. One thing was certain. Nothing and no one was going to rock the boat and take from him the little he had achieved!

Father spoke to the bank and to Victor Larsen, the solicitor, and bought a second-floor flat for himself on Nybrogade 9. There was a little balcony and a dining room, a living room, a bedroom and a kitchen, all just as it should be, and the only way he could afford it all was to go to auctions and wait for the lowest bid. He bought a dining table with four mahogany chairs, a genuine leather armchair, carpets and paintings that he hung in gilded frames – a country road with pollarded willows, a harbour with fishing boats, a forest scene – and his greatest coup was the grand piano. He couldn't play, but it was part of it all. Father even put sheet music on the stand for effect and the cleaner turned the pages once a week. Father relished his snug. He sat in the armchair reading German and English, dictionaries and grammar books mostly, and he applied to join the Brage male voice choir, went on outings to Pomlenakke and sang *How fresh and green the woodlands lie*. In the afternoons he could be seen crossing the Market Square carrying in his hands cakes from baker Jensen – two cream-filled angel cakes – making his calls and paying his respects to the ladies, even the married ones, and several cups of coffee later he was on his way back. They left him cold. He had his mother, and she cooked the food he liked and washed his clothes – that was all the woman he needed, and Father preferred to be left in peace. The icing on the cake came when he was allowed to join the Freemasons. He bought a tall hat and a dinner jacket and strutted off to lodge meetings on Wednesday evenings, and slowly he rose through the ranks and greeted the town's élite and carved out his career inch by inch.

Father constructed his existence around what meant more to him than anything else – security – and in the home he made for himself everything was perfectly ordered, while the world around him fell apart. Ib ended up in court, Annelise ran off with a man – and Father sorted it all out. It was always left to him to pick up the pieces. He was a character witness for Ib, who got off lightly with a suspended sentence, he made sure that Annelise came back home, and he found an apprenticeship for Leif with Balling & Sons (Hides, Skins & Leathers). He looked after his mother, who had got arthritis – no treatment helped – and helped his father, who was increasingly at his wit's end, not daring to walk the streets for fear of running into unpaid bills. They were due to move from 'Bellevue', now mortgaged to the hilt three or four times over – and Father sat up going over the paperwork into the small hours, while his father tore his hair and gabbled on about business and tourism and transport and routes as straight as the crow flies. There was no way out. They might just as well give up – they had reached the end of the line. Grandfather ran up and down the stairs looking to see where the future had got to. It had to be there soon! But it never came. It never came – and Karen took the kitchen clock off the wall, and the packing cases stood ready to be fetched, but they were empty. All was lost. And then it did come after all and was the worst thing that had ever happened.

It was on the morning of 9th April. Father and his little brother Ib were walking along Vesterskovvej – Ib's suit always looked rumpled even though it had just been pressed – and everywhere there were people shouting 'The Germans are coming! The Germans are coming!' As they stared up at the sky, the fighter squadrons flew north over the town. Ib threw a stone at them.

'What do we do now?'

'We go to work,' answered Father. 'What else?'

When something was wrong, he acted as though nothing had happened – and as a rule it worked. Father was reckoning he could ignore the Second World War and make it disappear.

People had gathered in the square, even those from the office. They stood talking, and Director Damgård told them that troops had come ashore. The word was that they were on their way from Gedser at that very moment. They had taken the ferry from Warnemünde that night.

'I hope they bought a bloody ticket an' all!' said Ib, laughing.

Father was beside himself that his brother should be shooting his mouth off and tried to get him to shut up, but Ib didn't give a damn. He said that the ferry should have been scuppered long since, and that the Germans wouldn't have had much bloody trouble navigating into the harbour when they had the lighthouse to guide them, and why hadn't anyone thought of turning it off?

'Ib!' shouted Father and was on the point of apologizing to Damgård and the others, but none of them said anything. There was nothing to be said. Ib was right, and they knew it.

Repairs on the road running north-south on Falster had been due for years. No one had done anything about it and the council's coffers were bare. But four days earlier the potholes had been filled in and the road was rolled and ready for use. The only bombardment that hit the invasion forces as they moved up through Gedesby, Bruserup and Marrebæk came from the signs saying '*Zimmer Frei*' and '*Potatoes for sale*'. The stallholders on the Market Square discussed whether they should draw down their shutters or display their goods with prices marked in Reichsmark. It was getting on for nine o'clock and it wouldn't be long before they reached Nykøbing. A German had been seen in Væggerløse and several more in Hasselø and Lindeskoven. They were on their way up Østergade and Nygade and Jernbanegade – and at that point reality overtook rumour. Soldiers arrived walking in columns, hugging the housefronts and covering both sides of the street with rifles at the ready. There was utter silence. Not a sound. And Father and Ib and the rest of them stood watching with gaping mouths, unable to believe their eyes, holding their breath, waiting for the influx that was approaching like rolling thunder, louder and louder, until it was just round the corner – and here was the German Army!

They marched right through the middle of the town –

infantrymen with knapsacks and helmets and rifles – tramping past, an endless sea of uniforms staring straight ahead. At the rear came the horse-drawn wagons carrying bread, but that was it – no tanks, no jeeps, not a single motorised vehicle. The blacksmith from the sugar factory could not resist and, as the last wagon clattered past, he tipped his cap and asked if the bread was for the horses. The soldier shook his head and said, *'Nein, für uns,'* and continued down Langgade and turned right into Rosenvænget. After twenty minutes the troops were back, their feet beating the same tempo as they marched up Kongensgade – and so they went round in circles.

Nykøbing was a tourist trap. The roads were one-way and each was a cul-de-sac. Once in, it was impossible to get out. The Germans had lost their way. With a bellow of *'Himmikruzifixherrgottsakrament!'*, the commanding officer snatched the map from the hands of a despairing adjutant, but it was no good. The invasion would have ended before it began, if it hadn't been for Father, who raised his hand.

'Entschuldigen Sie bitte,' he said, finding a use for his German at last. *'Kann ich Ihnen behilflich sein?'*

People stared at him as though he had gone crazy and would be shot on the spot. But Father went carefully across to the officers, greeting them politely and pointing at the map. They were to turn right at the Bjørnebrønd and Zaren's house and go past Holland's farm and down Slotsgade to Gåbensevej. They should not take the turning to Kraghave but continue down the road to Systofte and Tingsted and then continue along the A2 through Eskilstrup,

Nørre Alslev and Gåbense to the Storstrøm Bridge. From there the road went straight to Copenhagen, and Father wished them '*Gute Reise*'. They all waved from the Market Square and, when the last German soldier disappeared over the horizon, they could hear from the song of the blackbird how quiet things had become, how everything breathed out peace.

The Germans covered the 40 kilometres from Gedser to Masnedsund without a hitch and without the garrisons in Vordingborg and Næstved being alerted. Anyone would think that the Storstrøm Bridge had been built for them three years earlier. No one would have dreamt of blowing it up. There were two marines, both on national service, at the fort in Masnedø. They knew nothing about its artillery, so the German parachute troops had taken the bridge without a fight. Telegraph operators at railway stations in Nykøbing and later in Vordingborg, aware of the German advance, rang head office in Copenhagen to ask if they ought to report it to the military authorities. They were told to mind their own business and that's what they did – and that was also what my father planned to do, and the rest of Nykøbing with him.

The Second World War passed straight through the town and out the other side like a bullet that hit nothing and did no damage because it met with no resistance – and it was left to others to show the courage and the strength required to stand in the way. This was right up my father's street, and he was able to resume his daily duties at the office, to go on his excursions with the choir and to attend lodge meetings on Wednesdays as if nothing had happened. He breathed a sigh of relief and turned to Ib.

'Well, how about getting to work?' he said.

But Ib was gone.

I t was summer and the hedges were chirping, blue tits leapfrogged in the air, and Mother and Father and I sat eating lunch on the terrace. A lawnmower droned in the distance, and out on the road the girls jumped in hula hoops and skipped and peed their pants. Susanne had forget-me-not eyes and fair hair and freckles and all the children in kindergarten sang *Under the arches* and knew I was in love.

When I started at school, I would sit and write letters to her – will you? won't you? do you? don't you? – and fold the paper into envelopes that I never gave her. I hoped that she would say yes anyway, and at the party at the end of the first year we held hands and walked round and round the kiss that was waiting for me like a bee in a blackberry bush.

I cycled out to the beach, taking the main road that went up hill and down dale, heading straight out to where the larks would be singing above the sea-wall. There was the scent of pine and heather and salt water, and I lay there all day long thinking of Susanne and listening to the grasshoppers quivering and jigsawing their way through the stillness until Marielyst erupted in my ears and made my spine shiver with sheer delight.

S ex was the mysterious X and had no place in our family. I never saw my parents undressed – not once – and if it was ever mentioned on the radio when we were driving, they would immediately switch to another programme and pretend it hadn't happened. It was a no-go zone riddled with guilt and shame; just to mention it would be enough to get your hands chopped off at the table, and I'd be keeping well clear.

It was not just that it was unmentionable. It was also unthinkable, and I could not really form an idea of what it was. It was just round the corner, hiding under the bed and out in the dark, waiting for me, crouching, ready to attack me at any moment. I couldn't get it out of my head. Something was missing. There was an enigma, dangerous and forbidden, and when I was alone at home I went exploring without ever knowing what I was looking for.

We were visiting Grandmother in Frankfurt, and I took the chance to creep across to the bookshelves in the living room. They were massive and made of dark mahogany with cut glass in the doors, and they were full of books – Papa Schneider collected them. I started with the largest volume I could find that had pictures, leafing through Greek temples and Roman ruins and a world of flora and fauna – the flowers all coloured by hand – and then I started out on the encyclopaedia, *Der Große Brockhaus*. These were heavy books bound in black, dark-blue and gold, and they contained everything. *Jeden Tag ich Brockhaus preiss, denn er weiss, was ich nicht weiss,'* Mother said – and I was sure this was it when I came to the letter 'M' for 'man' and looked up *'Der Mensch'.*

There was an illustration of a naked woman. She was pink and there was not a hair on her body, not even on her head – she was bald – and you could unfold her to full length to include her legs and feet. She had breasts that you could open like doors in an advent calendar and showed what was concealed under the skin, her guts and her veins. Her flesh was as red as raw steak. I unfolded her stomach – it was just like opening the 24th December – and opened her up layer by layer and gazed at liver, intestines, heart. It was scary, and I quickly put the book back on the shelf – my conscience black as pitch – and could hardly wait until next time.

This gave me a taste for reading and I started going to the library in Nykøbing – a chalk-white building with a wide stairway. It was the most peaceful place on earth, it was on Rosenvænget and I left the town, the other children, everything behind me when I stepped in through the door. I ploughed my way through the rows of books in the children's section and, when I had emerged at the other end and shut the last book, I was old enough to set about the real task towering above me in the lofty room – the adult library.

The shelves went on forever, and for the first couple of years I could only reach the topmost ones with the aid of a stool. I followed my inclination, consulting the card index, looking for interesting titles, hunting among the bookshelves – and, even though I fought the temptation, slowly and surely I read my way in to the dangerous books, knowing full well where to find them: the *Sengeheste* series, Soya's novels, *Lady Chatterley*. I did not dare take them down. Simply skimming a passage or two demanded a steady nerve, a firm grip on my hammering heart. I was terrified of being caught. At long last I gave in, hid *Hvordan, mor?* under my sweater and read its revelations on the toilet. So there I sat cultivating the forbidden knowledge whenever I could – and felt so much at home out there that I stayed for hours and fell asleep.

It was inevitable. One day I overslept and, when I emerged from the toilet, it was long past closing time. The library was empty and dark as the grave. It was locked. I couldn't get out and was grabbed by panic, my pulse hammering in my throat. I was alone, a prisoner of the dark, and whatever would Mother and Father be thinking? They would be at their wits' end wondering where I had got to! I fumbled my way round the library as I remembered it – rows A, B, C – and my memory kept playing tricks on me, and I got more and more lost in the labyrinth of my own thoughts until I no longer knew where I was. I had walked into the trap – there was no way out, for the books went on forever – so I sat down and prayed that someone would find me before it was too late. The fluorescent lights flickered and caught. And there were Mother and Father walking in with the librarian. I leapt up and rushed to them, and it was a long while before I went out to the toilet again.

Autumn had arrived. I was on my way home from

school, walking under the bridge by the station and looking forward to the holidays. Torn pieces of paper were strewn like confetti across the pavement, shining in thousands of colours like leaves from the Garden of Eden, and I couldn't resist taking a look and peeling them off the slabs. They were easy to find because they glittered – more lay under the bushes and in the gutter – and I put them all in my school bag. When I arrived home, something stopped me in my tracks, and instead I turned my bike and rode out to Vesterskoven where, with the rooks screaming from the treetops, I dug a hole and buried the fragments of paper to save them for later.

It was an age before I could get down from the table and say 'thank you for the food' and ride back to the wood. I dug up the pieces of paper and then I put two and two together in pairs and started to assemble the jigsaw puzzle with a small roll of Sellotape. As it grew, so did my arousal, and slowly a picture took shape of what I could not have imagined in my wildest dreams. And I hadn't a clue where I was supposed to put it or what I was supposed to do with my secret once the last piece was taped into place and I found myself holding a dirty magazine in my hands: *Colour Climax, 1973.*

Mother was not to go and live with them in Kleinwanzleben until after the marriage had been consummated – as it was put – and Grandmother had given birth to a daughter with Papa Schneider. They hugged each other now and Grandmother wept, but they were miles apart, and from now on she would be the daughter of a previous marriage and come in second place after her stepsister, Eva. There was nothing to be done about it, so Mother patted the dog that was leaping about her – it was called Bello – and took her place in the Prussian upper-class like a guest moving into the others' lives.

Papa Schneider owned most of the district – the land, the people, the villages – and he walked around in riding boots and had the most magnificent motorcar, a Daimler-Benz. There were horses in the stables and servants. Mother was given her own room with a dressing-mirror and a wardrobe and a wide soft bed all to herself. She would never forget that first Christmas. There was the dinner, a tree full of candles, and she had been given everything – sledge, skis, dresses and picture-books. It was as if she had gone to heaven, Mother said, and she planned to keep her place there no matter what.

There was a daily drill, and times were as precise as the crack of a whip. At six o'clock in the morning: riding lessons. She was given the most skittish horse and rode around with a stick up her back and a book on her head, and God help you if it fell off. Then came French and English and piano until one o'clock, when Papa Schneider sat down at table. It would have been unthinkable to arrive late or for lunch not to be ready – it was sent up in the dumb waiter – ding! – and served as the hour struck. Nothing was said during the meal – or about the meal. You ate to live and did not live to eat! Afterwards Papa Schneider listened to the stock market report on the radio. The entire house held its breath and heaved a sigh of relief when it was over and he put on his coat and left, and Mother struggled through the remainder of the day, fighting to retain her place.

It was made clear from the start that she was illegitimate, that she was not a blood relative – *'blutsverwandt'* – as her sister was, and that she was to conduct herself accordingly. It wouldn't require many false moves to see her on her way. What was true for others was doubly true for Mother, and she did her homework and kissed Papa Schneider on the cheek – the left cheek with the scars – and made conversation in French and read English novels. She played the piano for Grandmother and her guests and performed the *Moonlight* sonata, her right foot pressing the sustain pedal to the floor. And Papa Schneider would watch as she rode at a gallop, taking the ditches as though she were on a hunt, though it was she who was the hunted quarry.

Mother played tennis, shrieked when she served and won tournaments – and the trophies on the shelf stood for one loss after the other. She wanted a hug from her mother and was given a coat. She wanted a father, and all she got was discipline of the old school, and she had to take what she could get and make the best of it. On his holidays Papa Schneider went fly-fishing in the Harz mountains, and Mother got up at half-past three in the morning and tagged along carrying his kit. If he forgot his hat after lunch, she ran after him, handing it to him with a *'Hier, Vati!'* The closest she got to him was when he stroked her hair and popped his hat on her head as a joke saying *'Kleiner Frechsack!'* and pinched her cheek so hard that she got a bruise, and Mother said that she was his and only his, and worked her way into him one smile at a time. She managed to carve out a place for herself – if not in his heart, at least in the car. And on Sundays they drove out into the blue yonder and folded down the hood and sang *Wochenend und Sonnenschein*. It felt almost like having a family, and she pressed herself against his side. Then they drove straight into the car in front and Mother went clean through the windscreen.

She sat there with blood streaming from a face that was cut to shreds – just like his – and in reality maybe this was why Papa Schneider accepted her after the accident. She was given the best treatment money could buy at the university clinic in Vienna, and the cuts healed without leaving scars – except around her one eye, Mother always pointed out, and I nodded even though I could see nothing – and he took her under his wing, put her photograph in his wallet and became a different person. Mother was allowed to do almost anything – and did. She had boyfriends and made trouble and, when she came home with Stichling, who was ten years older than her, she even got away with that. Papa Schneider forgave her everything. She was the only person who could sweeten him when he lost his temper. She could talk him into anything, and, if she had spent too much money, he would laugh and say, *'Motto Hilde: Immer druf!'* And maybe that was Mother's motto: *Don't stop there!*

Papa Schneider loved her more than the horses, loved her as much as he was able to love anyone, and Mother was included in the family portrait alongside his dog. They were on an outing in the countryside. Grandmother was sitting in the grass with Eva in her arms, Papa Schneider was reading a book, and Mother had on a short dress – it was almost transparent – and a pageboy haircut. She was standing next to Bello looking out at me from the painting in the dining room when we sat down to eat, and Mother told me that it had been painted by Magnus Zeller. He was one of the expressionists from the München group, *Der Blaue Reiter*. Papa Schneider supported him and bought his pictures – he was also a patron of Max Pechstein and Emil Nolde. They had all hung on the walls until 1937, when he had been forced to take them down – they were what Hitler called 'degenerate art' – and he rolled them up and hid them in the cellar. While Nolde's fear led him to paint flowers, Pechstein and Zeller took up landscape painting. Two of them hung in heavy gold frames in our living room – one of mountains and flowing water in the Harz mountains, where Papa Schneider went on his fishing trips, and another of some sombre trees by a lake. The others had been taken by Auntie Eva – and that was not the end of it. She had taken everything.

It was just like in the fairytale. The stepsister was evil, and Mother had grown up with a snake that grew more poisonous with every year that passed. Eva was fat and ugly and red-haired, and even though she never had to achieve anything and had everything served up on a plate, it fell through her fingers and shattered around her. She was put on a circus horse and fell off and never got on again. She was as tone deaf as a set of bagpipes and conjugated French verbs out of all recognition. Eva was father's little girl and was sat on his knee and applauded for nothing, but it was no good. On the contrary it made the worm of envy turn more viciously in her whenever she hit the ball into the net and she watched Mother walk round in her tennis skirt being everything that she was not – beautiful and popular. Mother dressed her in smart clothes, put her hair up and took her along to parties when she became a teenager. Eva was a wallflower and her birthday parties attracted only bores. To inject a bit of life into it, Mother made a punch and dished it out, and the party took off. They let their hair down, laughing and dancing and behaving like wild things, chasing up and down the house, and Eva kissed a boy – and the party was over. One of the guests fell over and fainted and had to be taken to hospital because he had a dicky heart. Mother had put speed in the punch, and she got Eva to swear and cross her heart and hope to die that she would not tell a soul – and then the snake struck.

Mother was sent away to the best girls' boarding school that could be found, Reinhardswaldschule outside Kassel. It was built on a hill looking out across the town, and the main building was surrounded by a park, by the long dormitory buildings and by a wall. The gate was locked. This was where royalty, the aristocracy and big industrialists sent their daughters to keep them out of trouble, and her school friends were called Sayn-Wittgenstein and Thüssen and Thurn and Taxis. The principal made a point of it when he came to Mother's name, saying it aloud at morning assembly:

'Hildegard Lydia ... Voll!' She still bore her father's name – she had never been adopted – and it was just as embarrassing as being illegitimate. Mother ran and rode and jumped and beat them at tennis and played the piano and provided entertainment when they had evenings off, and that would have to compensate for lack of family and title.

Outside the school the world was a dangerous place. They were not allowed to go into town, and most forbidden of all were cinemas and cafés – not to mention the '*Tanzcafé*' which had music and dance and, worst of all, men. Men belonged in another world and were the closest you could get to dying. Every other Saturday the girls were driven in a bus with blacked-out windows to a *Konditorei* that had been closed to the public for the occasion. There they ate cakes, drank tea and made polite conversation, while their teachers perched like blackbirds observing them, and there was no music. They had to be in bed – with the lights out – at ten o'clock, but Mother smuggled gramophone records into the dormitory and held midnight parties. She would stick a pencil through the hole in the middle, and they would turn the record with their fingers, stick a matchstick with a piece of greaseproof paper in the grooves and listen to the latest hits – *Benjamin, ich hab' nichts anzuzieh'n* – and, when they got to the final exams, Mother and her best friend, Inge Wolf, bunked off and went to the cinema. They hid among the padded chairs and cried so much they didn't know what had hit them, and afterwards they sat smiling with red-rimmed eyes, aching and dizzy and tender all over.

Mother got away from Reinhardswaldschule in 1939 and

went to Berlin to study at the university – political science and American history – and there she met Horst Heilmann and fell in love. He was nineteen like her and called her '*Hildchen*', and she called him '*Horstchen*', and Mother threw herself into his arms, opened her heart and was given back the life that had been taken away from her before it had begun. They were engaged when the war broke out, and Horst entered the *Wehrmacht*, where he was given the task of breaking codes for intelligence in Berlin, while Mother did her student service as a tram conductor – her 'Studiendienst' – and was photographed in uniform and used for propaganda because she was young and blonde: *'Deutsche Mädel stehen überall ihren Mann. Front und Heimat Hand in Hand!'*[1] She posed as a conductor in *Der Silberspiegel* and as a gymnast in *Reichssportblatt* – '*Frisch und froh!*' She was a pin-up in bathing suit in the SS magazines that did the rounds of the front line, so that Mother's conquests included Belgium, Holland, France, Tunisia. It gave them a good laugh, Mother and Horst, and they passed the magazines around, reading the captions aloud when they were with his friends – Kuckhoff, who was in the theatre, and Harro Schulze-Boysen, who taught foreign affairs at the university and made himself out to be a Nazi even though he was a fervent anti-fascist. His wife, whose name was Libertas, was employed by Metro-Goldwyn-Mayer, and they watched American movies – *Gone with the Wind* – and listened to allied radio stations. At night they posted flyers

[1] All German girls stand by their man. Front and homeland hand in hand!

and hung posters up – '*Das Nazi-Paradies. Krieg, Hunger, Lüge, Gestapo. Wie lange noch?*'[2] – and Harro carried a gun. They pinned their hopes on the USA and the Soviet Union and prayed that one day would see an end to it, and so it did.

In the autumn of 1942 Mother went on holiday to occupied Paris with Inge Wolf, and when she returned to Berlin Horstchen was not at home. She rang Harro and Libertas. There was no answer. No answer from Kuckhoff, nor from anyone else in their circle. Mother rushed over to the last person who to her knowledge knew Horstchen. Liane lived in Berlin-Schøneberg on Viktoria-Luise-Platz. She was at home and let Mother in and was in a state of total confusion. They had been arrested, the lot of them, Arvid Harnack and his wife, Mildred, Günter Weisenborn, John Graudenz – more than a hundred of them. Mother's head swam, she was in shock and ran back to her room and began ringing the authorities to ask what had happened to Horst, Horst Heilmann, her beloved Horst! No one could tell her. At his workplace she was just told that he was away on official business, a '*Dienstreise*', and, instead of giving her information, the police interrogated her. Who was she? What connections did she have to these people? In the end she got hold of Himmler's secretary, sobbing down the telephone and asking where her Horstchen was and what had they done? It felt as if there was no one at the other end, as if the voice came from the void.

[2] This Nazi paradise. War, hunger, lies, Gestapo. How much longer?

'Er ist verhaftet und wird vernommen, Sie haben sich beim Volksgerichtshof einzufinden, und zwar sofort. Heil Hitler!'[3]

She struggled to understand. Horstchen under arrest? And she was to appear before the court? Against all better reasoning Mother went, ran up the stairs and down the corridors, until she saw the guards marching towards her with a man. It was Horst! She called his name, and he looked up. He was in handcuffs, and they dragged him past her – there was nothing Mother could do – she only heard Horstchen whisper from a great distance.

'Flee, Hildchen. Flee!'

Mother had no idea where she should flee, did not dare return to Victoria Studienanstalt but did so anyway, and, when she returned home, Papa Schneider was standing in her room with a coat over his arm and a suitcase packed. He had done everything in his power to ensure that it was not the Gestapo who would be waiting for her. There was no time to lose – Horst Heilmann was accused of high treason and she was in mortal danger and had to disappear immediately. He handed her money and papers and an envelope with a letter in case she got into difficulties, and Mother thanked him and wept and left for Graz. She could think of nothing but Horstchen, who was gone, and the abyss opened up inside her and never closed again.

---

[3] He is under arrest and will be interrogated. You are to report to the People's Court and to do so at once. Heil Hitler!

I had only one wish on my birthday and that was not to have a birthday, and I lay awake the night before imagining time leapfrogging the day without anyone noticing it so it would never happen, and then I walked into the dining room where Mother and Father would be singing

Knüdchen hat Geburtstag, tra-la-la-la-la!
Knüdchen hat Geburtstag, heisa-hopsa-sa!

There would be ring cake with candles – a *Gugelhupf* – and toffees round my plate and presents from Grandmother and the Hagenmüller family and from Auntie Gustchen and Auntie Inge, who lived on Majorca and sent many happy returns and 10 Deutschmarks. I was given everything Mother and Father could give – a bicycle, an Optimist dinghy and a moped when I was fifteen – and it would all be taken away from me during the course of the day and punctured or sunk or destroyed. When I blew out the candles and opened the last package all I hoped was that it would be a bomb and would bring on the end of the world.

It was always too much and so wrong. Father had brought the bicycle back from Germany, had bought it at Neckermann with the slogan '*Neckermann macht's möglich!*', though it wasn't clear what they made possible. It had wide white tyres and no one north of the Alps rode a bike like it. I knew in advance that the tyres would have been let down when I rode home from school and I could wheel it home and repair it and keep on repairing it until I gave up. I was covered in shame when I stood up in class and the words 'Knud's birthday' were written on the blackboard, and Miss Kronov had said that I would now hand round sweeties. The idea was that you would go round with a tin of boiled sweets and everyone would take one. Mother had spent a whole week filling little cellophane bags with liquorice and wine gums and home-made chocolates and tied bows around them. When I handed them round the class, they all made faces and then they sang, exploding in laughter when they finished off their 'Happy birthday to Knud' with 'Heisa-hopsa-sa!' The worst was to come. I handed round the rest of the bags in the break and invited them to my birthday party. Then it was over and I was left more or less in peace while they ate sweets, until they threw up and asked if there were any more and said, 'See ya, then!'

I was beside myself with terror when the time came and they rang the bell and came through the front door, one, two, three at a time dropping a five-crown coin in my hand – it wasn't wrapped up and that was what people gave in 1970. With twenty in the class that made 100 crowns. There was no way around it. I had to let them in – Pia and Jeanne and Marianne and Georg and Kim and Michael and Jesper and Lisbet and Annemette and Jens-Erik and Poul and Jørgen and the rest of them. They had come to celebrate my birthday, and they all had one thing on their mind – to have a cheap laugh at our expense and tell their parents about it afterwards. And they got what they came for.

Mother had laid the table in the dining-room – white tablecloth, place cards and flags, balloons and candles – and beside each plate lay a package with presents – crayons, marbles, picture lotto – and she smiled and said, 'So, Kinder, now sit you down and have a good enjoyment!' She served up hot waffles and *Spritzkuchen* and *Kartoffelpuffer* with apple preserve, and they stared at it all and looked around for all the things they were used to – the buttered rolls that weren't there, the banana layer cake that wasn't there, the soda pop that had been swapped for Nesquick. They wouldn't enjoy a single mouthful, that was for sure. They sat there, stabbing and spoiling and spilling on the floor, and they burst the balloons and drew on the table-cloth and sniggered and couldn't wait for Mother to start on the entertainment. She had organized competitions, and we played *Blindekuh* and *Wettfischen* and *Mäusejagd* and *Papiertütenlauf*, and they could throw balls at cans and there were prizes for everyone.

'Auf die Plätze, fertig – los!'

And 'Ready, steady, go!' they started – making fun and hurling balls, making Mother run around picking them up while they grabbed what they could and filled their pockets with sweets. I pretended I didn't hear them teasing and putting on a German accent and calling me *'Knüdchen'* like Mother did, slapping each other on the back, breathless with laughter. The important thing was to get through the day. No matter what I did, I could not avoid the catas-trophe waiting ahead – it was an annual tradition – and I shuddered at the thought that it would soon be evening and time for Mother to bring out her accordion. Father kept himself in the background, and they assembled in the street outside and were each given a long stick with a paper shade and a candle hanging inside. There were lanterns of all colours and with moons and stars and mysterious faces that shone in the darkness. Then we shuffled into a long line, and Mother began playing birthday songs, singing *'Knüdchen hat Geburtstag, tra-la-la-la-la'*, and slowly we set off, Pia and Jeanne and Marianne and Georg and Kim and Michael and Jesper and Lisbet and Annemette and Jens-Erik and Poul and Jørgen and me and all the others. We walked down Hans Ditlevsensgade and up Peter Freuchensvej and round the estate, Mother with her accordion at the head now singing *'Laterne, Laterne, Sonne, Mond und Sterne'* – and wherever we went people stood outside their houses and followed the procession and raised their right arm in a Hitler salute.

It was inconceivable that Mother did not notice – she knew perfectly well what was going on but she did it anyway. Her will was hard as steel and cold as ice and shone out of her cold and steel-grey eyes. She had been through things that were worse, had played her accordion to accompany the apocalypse. It was in 1945 at the end of the war, after Mother had given up any hope of finding her family and had cycled out to the German army outside Magdeburg to find something to eat. She was given soya beans, and they found out that she had been to university, was an academic translator working with English, and that was something they would soon be needing. In no time she found herself part of the *Volkssturm*, the Nazi militia, and set off with the remnants of the 9th Army under General Raegener –

15,000 soldiers, the young, the old, the wounded, going to the Führer's rescue in *Festung Berlin*. But they were cut off by the Russians and there was no escape. Their only hope was to capitulate to the Americans, and in desperation they fought their way out, moving westwards and northwards, and managed to reach the second front. General Raegener, who had a wooden leg, sat in a bunker with his adjutant and with Mother, who played *Guter Mond, du gehst so stille* as the bombs howled and thundered down around them, and then it was over. She got out alive, and when Mother rounded the corner and made it back to Hans Ditlevsensgade and stopped outside our house with her accordion over her shoulders and children and neighbours trailing behind her in a stream of shining lanterns, she sang louder than ever and dragged the final chord out further and further until all of them and the houses, the streets, the whole town, were sucked into the bellows and disappeared, and Mother and Father and I stood alone with each other and celebrated my birthday with a *'heisa-hopsa-saaa!'*

There was no television – Mother and Father called it the idiot box. We never went to the cinema – I didn't even know there was one in town – and cartoons were out of the question because they made you stupid. Compared to books, they were trash, immoral almost, and relegated to the back page of the newspapers like the *Phantom* in *The Lolland-Falster Times*. It was language, above all the written word, that could express intelligence and wit, and when I saw comic books laid out on the table in the library – *Tintin*, *Lucky Luke*, *Asterix* – I didn't dare open them. I was afraid that a single peek would be enough, that I would never be the same again, that I would become an idiot, get a harelip, be changed beyond recognition. I borrowed books and read. Otherwise our only entertainment at home was the card games, board games, dice games, and we sat around the dining table in the afternoons playing *Whist* and *Räubers Rommy* and *Mensch Ärgere Dich Nicht* and *Yatzy*. The grandfather clock ticked. Their lives were mine, and I had nothing of my own. But that changed overnight when I got my own radio.

It was a little silver Philips transistor, and I sat with my ear glued to it from the moment I pressed 'on'. There was only medium-wave and short-wave, and it wasn't very powerful, but I had found a way through. The signals reached Hans Ditlevsensgade, and the world opened up before me. Father asked me to turn it down straight away, of course, and I turned down the sound and lay there at night holding my breath and listening in the dark. The sounds came crackling and foaming in between bursts of Tyrolean and Turkish music as I scrolled the wheel backwards and forwards, always thirsty for more. Voices and snatches of tunes and snips of Morse mingled and gathered into a mesh of weird music, and the next day there were dark circles under my eyes because I had not slept.

My radio gave me my first chance to get away from Mother and Father, to be able to follow my own desires and decide for myself, and it felt as if what I was doing was forbidden. I hid under my duvet so as not to be discovered and explored all earthly space, listening to its secrets. Radio stations emerged from white noise, Westdeutscher Rundfunk, ORF, Voice of America and 'This is the BBC World Service'. Unknown broadcasts were constantly breaking in and interfering. Russian newsreaders and military music took over from German folk singers and American news. There was a sea of voices that drowned each other out – and I was on the track of something, was searching without knowing what I was searching for, until it exploded in my ears on 208 kHz: Radio Luxemburg!

It was the most beautiful thing I had ever heard and utterly impossible to resist. There was music and commercial spots and jingles and sound effects and people ringing in from Amsterdam and Düsseldorf, and the disc jockey – Rob Jones – spoke so fast that you couldn't keep up with his fluid and melodic voice announcing the next number. I heard Sweet and Slade and Wings and Queen and Sparks and couldn't believe it was true, but it was, and I had escaped from the nineteenth century and arrived in 1974. Sweeter than anything I had ever heard, the sounds sparkled and glittered. Nothing was the same anymore, and I couldn't wait for the clock to strike eight and the broadcast to begin.

I lived for Radio Luxemburg in another world that existed only on the radio and at night. This was a far cry from *Ask Århus* and *Record Request* coming out of the transistor in the kitchen or the traffic reports that Father used to plague me with when we drove down to fetch Mother in Frankfurt – she would visit Grandmother a couple of times a year – and on the motorway I would get bored and begged and bullied him to change programme. The further south we got the better the chance of picking up the American forces station – AFN – and I drank in the sound of the radio hosts and the music and the adverts as if it were Coca-Cola for the few minutes that Father let them play before he groaned and retuned because it was just noise. This was the modern world, and we left it behind us for good and all when we arrived at the Westend in Frankfurt towards evening. There were large chestnut trees and large town houses with casement windows and balconies, and Grandmother lived in an apartment on Kettenhofweg 106, where time had stopped, or had been bombed and blown to pieces and left for dead.

I leapt from the car, gave Mother a hug and kissed Grandmother, and she wept for joy, as she usually did, and we went upstairs with the bags and unpacked. Then we sat down to eat, and I was given '*Schinken-Kren*' – pale rye-bread spread with fat and covered with thin rolled slices of ham with egg and pickled cucumber with horseradish over the top – and my eyes smarted so much at the horserad-ish that the tears trickled down my cheeks. Grandmother handed me her damp handkerchief and smiled her lipless smile. Her hands had been ravaged and were covered with the same horny skin as her face. She was still on fire, and the Second World War haunted the living rooms and shivered in the glass door leading out to the hall – to the horror, the madness, the shame – and when I was sent to bed and lay in the darkness and heard an aeroplane approach and fly over the house, I would be frightened that the war had started again, that the bombs would start falling, and I would search for Radio Luxemburg.

There were golden moments when the signal came clear as a bell. As a rule there would be atmospheric noise, and I'd just found Luxemburg in my bedroom at Grandmother's when the spookiest sound drowned it out. A woman's voice reading out numbers – empty and monotonous and never-ending. *'Achtung. Achtung,'* she said and counted *'1,2,3,4,5,6,7,8,9,0'* – *'Eins, Zwei, Drei …'* and so on. This was followed by Austrian folk music with a yodeller, and then it all started again and went on. I knew immediately what it was, and a shiver went up my spine. It was the Cold War, and the numbers were a code sending secret messages to spies.

They were everywhere on short and medium wave, German and English and Russian transmitters, and there was a lonely woman's voice saying over and over again *'Papa November, Papa November'* for five minutes on end while a frantic snake-charmer flute played in the background, and then she started to rattle off numbers in German, *'406, 422, 438, 448, 462'* – and there were other stations that had names like Papa Zulu, Charlie November, Sierra Tango or Foxtrot Bravo. Some of them had their own signature tune, like the English one that started with the first bars of a folk song before a woman with an English accent read off rows of numbers, or the Spanish station with lousy studio reverb where you could occasionally hear a cock crow. The scariest of them all played a few notes on a musical box and then after a while a girl's voice would begin reciting numbers in a sweet and innocent German.

What could make anyone use a child to read out messages to secret agents? Where did such things go on? And who were these people sitting with their radios somewhere or other in Europe writing the numbers down? There must be women walking around among us whose job it was to intone columns of numbers, year in, year out without being allowed to tell anyone. Who were they? What was going on? I could go into a trance listening to the numbers weaving between the interference from jamming stations and the music. The voices of the women mingled with the sound of the aeroplane flying over the house on Kettenhofweg and with the fear of the Second World War, of the bombs that never stopped falling and that hit Grandmother every night. These were the nursery rhymes that I heard on the radio and to which I fell asleep during the Cold War.

Aunt Ilse had a hatred of cats, and this she shared with her nearest and dearest, a dachshund and a canary. They meant the world to her – she was childless – and her husband, who was placed well beneath her pets in the hierarchical order, had no say in the matter. His name was Heinrich Jaschinski – or Dr Jaschinski, as he was known – and he was director of the Deutsche Bank in Frankfurt. It was never quite clear to me which side of the family Aunt Ilse belonged to, but she was ugly as sin and sour as old milk and devoted her life to making life a misery for everyone else – especially her husband. He was well-to-do and influential and sailed about in a Mercedes as big and black as a battleship, but as soon as Ilse entered the room he would curl up in his shell. Her dachsund would scurry across and bite at his shoe, and, when he tried to ward it off, she would explode. *'Heinrich!'* And he would wither and disappear before your eyes.

Aunt Ilse was the eldest of three sisters. The others were beautiful and had married early – unlike her. She turned bitter when her first sister acquired a husband, and as the years passed she became more and more eaten up with vindictiveness and hate. No one would have her. And at her second sister's wedding the floodgates of resentment burst. Ilse spilt a glass of red wine down the bride's wedding dress before the service, did so on purpose and didn't even pretend to be sorry. If she could not find happiness, then the least she could do was to ruin it for others, and Ilse turned into a witch.

When at last they managed to find a husband for her, it was too late. Heinrich Jaschinski, whose family came from Stettin and had nothing to their name, only married her so that he could afford to go to university and complete his studies. No one was under any illusions about it, not even Aunt Ilse herself, who made sure they all got what they deserved. She became uglier than ever, pursed her mouth up, tied her bun tighter and stopped shaving the wart on her chin. She put too much salt in the food, terrified the children and poisoned the atmosphere whenever she could. *'Ach, Ilsekind,'* Grandmother would say to her with a sigh, but she wouldn't change her ways and was always ordering people about, bitching about them and tearing strips off Heinrich. Then she would scratch the canary and call it *'Piep-matz'*, her voice as rasping as the biscuits she fed it with.

There were more rules in the Jaschinski household than in algebra, and Mother instructed me in advance in what I was and was not to do and in how I was to conduct myself. I was put into a suit, and it was 'Yes, Aunt Ilse' and 'Thank you, Dr Jaschinski' – and the most important thing of all was not to make the canary nervous. That was why you mustn't wear any yellow, for that got it excited. It perched in its cage never making a sound, and I awaited my moment. As soon as Aunt Ilse got up and left the room, I pulled out a yellow handkerchief, waved it about and blew my nose – and the bird went mad. It chirruped and screeched and wouldn't stop, while the dachshund ran round and round barking and biting the carpet. Ilse followed us to the door, ranting and raging, and I held out my hand and said sorry to her husband and saw the shadow of a smile touch his lips.

Aunt Ilse plagued the life out of Heinrich Jaschinski, who died many years before she did. Or rather, he did not die but wasted away, turning to dust, to a ghost – and, as ghosts do, he took his revenge from the grave. The entire family was gathered at the solicitor's, each sitting on tenterhooks waiting for the will to be read out, when a single woman walked in, took off her hat, sat down in a corner by herself and smiled shyly – and Ilse grew paler and paler with every word that was spoken. Because she had not fulfilled her nuptial obligations – not on one single occasion, not even on their wedding night – he had felt himself obliged to look elsewhere. He disinherited Ilse, and she got only what she was entitled to by law – her jewellery, the house and 8 per cent. His secretary would inherit instead, receiving half his estate. The rest went to the Cat's Protection League.

The winter months and the view across endless fields had given Farmor a sense for drama, and to make things even more scary she would light the candles and lower her voice as she related how Carl always used to follow his mother across the courtyard with the candle lantern when he was little. They lived at the tannery, which was situated on the edge of town and was built round three sides of a courtyard. It was a dark and desolate place, and there was every reason to be frightened since it lay right up against the churchyard. Then she would begin her ghost story.

It all started when the circus came to Nykøbing in the eighteenth century – and the fact that we were called Romer was because the circus manager was Italian. The horses fell ill, the performance was cancelled, and he was stranded on Falster. He could not buy new horses for the money he could get for the dead. The prices were so low that he kept them, slaughtered and skinned them himself and set himself up in the town as a tanner.

It was foul work separating skin from flesh and fat to make leather, and knackers were ostracized like prostitutes or hangmen. They were pariahs, and whoever he married, the girl could only be pitied. It was a hellish inferno of rotting carcasses, skeletons, skins and fire. The stench of sulphur rose from the pits from dawn till dusk. There were so many rats that their runs could make the buildings collapse into rubble, and the effluent dyed the river red with blood. They had five children, though love played no part in that, and two of them gave up the struggle in their first year. They called them angel children, and they were better off than those who remained behind on earth.

Their children grew up in a playpen made out of stripped ribs. They played with death and worked as soon as they could walk. There was nowhere for them to go, since the town was forbidden territory – and when the time came to find an apprenticeship, there was nothing for them. They were unclean, outcast and the only option for them was to carry on the family business and take over the yard, and so the knacker's yard went from father to son for over a hundred years, until it was Grandfather's turn in 1898.

Carl did the unthinkable and said no, refusing to take the business on. He did not want to be a knacker, fought against his fate with all the hope and courage and dynamism he had in him, sitting up all night reading the newspapers, keeping abreast of the times, learning about foreign parts and making his plans. He skinned the animals, washed the skins and dreamed all the while of leaving it all as far behind as possible. When his parents died, he sold the yard, put the contents up to auction – and then he put on his Sunday best and proposed to Karen.

But no matter what Grandfather touched, it went wrong, and everywhere he was dogged by black misfortune. Time and again he was cheated or played for high stakes, and each time he only dug the hole deeper for himself. He spent all he had – first all the proceeds from the sale of the yard and then, when they had been used up, he blew Karen's inheritance. Now there was nothing left, and they were forced to leave their house and home, move out of 'Bellevue', and all that remained of the knacker's yard were a knife and a kettle – and the candle lantern.

It stood on the table, burning and sending shadows from another century across the walls of the living room. Farmor smiled into the darkness. She had finished telling her story. I could hear the ticking of the grandfather clock – and, as the silence gathered and time stood still and the ghosts waited at the door, she whispered that a curse hung over our family. Then she blew out the candle and was gone. And I had never met her – she died before I was born – and the hairs stood up on the back of my neck.

Farmor and Grandfather ended up in a terraced bungalow on Søvej, where there was no room for the grand visions of 'Bellevue' – you had to open the window to see further than the end of your own nose, Carl used to say – and he resigned himself and took a job with Danish Railways. He was shadow of his former self, and when he crossed the tracks on his way to work, he kept his eyes shut. A train ran over him every time he thought of Canada, of the hotel, of the buses or of Marielyst. There was nothing he had ever believed in that had not ended in failure – none of his dreams had got them anywhere. As if that were not bad enough, he survived long enough to witness the success of others, as business and tourism took off, and Marielyst flourished. It was the worst punishment he could have been given, to see the trains coming and going – to Amsterdam, Berlin, Paris, Rome – people travelling the world, while he stood on the platform whistling and waving his flag, and was left behind in Nykøbing.

He would have liked to have sold everything, to have taken Karen away with him as far as they could go for the money, and then to have lain down to die at the end of the road – the wish was born of despair – but he bit back the urge, said not a word but clipped tickets and collected his wages. And each day that passed his headache grew. It felt as though everything was bearing down on him, was wanting to get out – all the good ideas, the fine intentions, the rosy prospects that had never turned into anything but dust – and he could not think a thought without it causing him pain. There was a whining in his ears, and he would cross the tracks after work and stay there, waiting for the train – he counted to a hundred, to two hundred and on up – and when he came home he would sit down at the table, eat, kiss Farmor and say thank you, knowing all the time that it was only a matter of time.

It was not until his eyes were popping out of his head

that he gave in to the pain and told Father – something wasn't quite right – and was sent to hospital. It was the worst place in town. The doctors didn't have a clue and came up with a diagnosis that was not simply wrong – it was vindictive. Syphilis. Karen wept, and even though she believed him and knew that it was not possible – he loved her more than all the world – the humiliation was not to be borne, and Grandfather spend his last days being ashamed of something that he had not done. He was driven off to be examined at the clinic for sexually transmitted diseases in Copenhagen, where they only needed to take one look at him to know what was wrong. Carl was transferred immediately to the State Hospital, where they could tell him that he had a brain tumour and three weeks left to live – and those weeks were used by the doctors to carry out a trial. He was injected with chemicals, irradiated and encased in a huge cylinder that spun him round and round and round and away into death.

Carl gave up the ghost in 1949 and was buried in Østre churchyard, which looked out onto the Sugar Factory – to the site where the knacker's yard had once stood. It had long since been demolished. It was an irony of fate that fourteen years later a direct rail route was opened connecting Berlin and Copenhagen – just as he had foreseen. It was christened Fugleflugtslinjen and, true to its name, sent trains straight as the crow flies, right past his grave. But it shouldn't make us sad, Farmor said. It had all ended well. Grandfather had only ever wanted one thing and that was to get away, and now his wish had been granted.

The road to freedom was packed with refugees hauling children and old relatives and as many things as they could carry, and Mother felt ashamed sitting in an American jeep overtaking them all. Then she thought of her mother – and of Papa Schnieder, Eva, her cousin Inge – and joy bubbled up inside her. They were alive and in the West! They had survived the war, all of them, and she was on her way home and had been such a long way away that it was almost too good to be true.

Raegener Division had been annihilated by the 2nd US Armoured Division and the 30th US Infantry Division, and Mother crawled out of her bunker on 18th April 1945. She acted as translator during the capitulation and was sent to a camp for prisoners of war. Germany may have fallen to the Americans, but the American GIs fell for Mother. She played cat and mouse with them, stroking an arm here, smiling there and throwing back her hair until in the end they gave her a Red Cross uniform that would get her out of the camp. She didn't bat an eyelid but went straight to the hospital in the sector, Magdeburg-Goslar, and reported for duty as a nursing orderly.

Mother tended the sick and the wounded and the dying, but it was hopeless. She couldn't bear it. For as soon as they recovered, the soldiers were fetched and driven back to the Russians as prisoners of war on the other side of the Elbe. The whole area was going to be handed over to the Soviet Union the following month and the only thing to do was to get away, but she hung in there, waiting to hear from her family and to find her mother. She set enquiries in motion through the Red Cross, and, when the news came, she could hardly believe her luck. They had been evacuated to Einbeck!

She gave the head of the sector – Mr Plaiter – a kiss and got leave from the hospital. Then she wiped her mouth, picked up her suitcase and persuaded an American soldier to drive her to Einbeck – Papa Schneider was rich, he would be well paid for his trouble, and it was only 190 kilometres. When they drew up in the courtyard, she jumped out. It was Eva who caught sight of her first and shouted *'Hilde!'*, and the others came running, and she wept and laughed and kissed them and threw her arms around Papa Schneider and asked for her mother. Where was she?

The figure that lay in the bed was a mummy, and she blacked out, broke down, strangling her screams, unable to breathe. Grandmother had been caught in an air raid that hit their house in Magdeburg as she was sorting out the washing in the cellar. The containers full of white gas in the room next door exploded, and she went up in flames. Mother wanted to kiss her, to stroke her hair, but she had no hair and no skin and was seared with pain at the slightest touch, by a breath of wind even. They kept the windows closed and crept around, carefully opening the doors, and every movement was torture. She stared out from under her bandages and her eyes were begging to die. And Mother gathered her whole life into one look – *'Ich bin bei dir'* – and whispered it so softly that it could scarcely be heard. *I am with you.*

Papa Schneider gave his camera to the soldier who had driven Mother home, and then there was nothing left. His wife, his estate, his land, he had lost it all – and now they were refugees in their own country, and not even welcome at that. They had been brought to this farm outside Einbeck, Kuhlgatzhof – now dilapidated, it dated from 1742 and had belonged to a snaps distiller – where they now lived in what had been one of the living rooms, with table and chairs and one camp bed each. In the room next door they had installed Fräulein Zilvig, who was a churchgoer. And then there was Frau Rab, who stole. The daughter of the Kuhl-gatz family lived on the second floor and was married to an artist, Herr Hänsel, and they lived with Frau Dömicke, who was the widow of a doctor and dressed in old-fashioned clothes. Herr Webendürfer had previously been the manager of a fridge factory and had his quarters out in the stable. He had been a student in a duelling club and was always demanding satisfaction and rattling his sabre – *'Ich verlange Satisfaktion!'* His plump and freckled daughter was called Oda and in the midst of it all she gave birth to a child and squealed like a stuck pig.

'Ach, Kinder, ihr seid nichts als Vieh,' Papa Schneider snorted and informed them that they had sunk to the level of beasts.

Herr Hänsel had a servant girl, Schmidtchen, who was a refugee from Pomerania and had a little daughter. She was slow-witted but did her best to make herself useful, fishing in the river and digging for worms in the dung-heap. Then she went off leading a she-goat to have her tupped and when she returned she stank of he-goat – and so did the stairs, the living rooms, everything – and it hung in the air no matter how much they scrubbed and scoured. It was too much for Herr Hänsel, who could no longer control his urges, and Mother was constantly having to say no and to ward off his advances, which became more and more physical. She didn't give a fig for the artist or for the Expressionist daubs he painted and hung along the corridor outside the toilet. And when she had been to the bathroom she would genuflect before his self-portrait and say, *'Meister, ich habe gespült'*.

Frau Dömicke's son had suffered brain-damage from shell-fire and was missing a section of his skull. When he took off his hat, you could see the blood pumping round and his brain mass pulsating. He was mad – and madly in love with Eva, who had an admirer at last, but it was the bane of their lives. It ended up with him assaulting her and hauling her behind a bush, but she escaped and ran home weeping and screaming that she wanted to get away, to get back to Kleinwanzleben, wanted everything to be as it had been before!

Mother fetched milk from the nearby farm, Mönchshof – they had ration coupons for three litres a week. To get to the cowshed, she had to pass a goose, which stood chained to the entrance and hissed at her. One day something went wrong and the goose was loose, flapping its wings and beating and biting until the farmhand came running to the rescue. Mother had fainted and was carried back to the farm, where prisoners were airing the place out. They had carried tables and chairs out into the open and were beating the carpets – and they put her to bed. She had bruises all over her body and was sick and vomiting, but the only medical man in the vicinity was the vet. He told her that she had broken two ribs – and that she might be … pregnant? He beat his arms up and down and laughed – it was only a joke – and gave her morphine. She had had enough of life on the farm.

More refugees kept arriving all the time, from Pomerania, from Lithuania, and Papa Schneider sank into black depression. Mother tried to comfort him, while at the same time she nursed Grandmother, looked after Eva and Inge and struggled on. And she determined that she would get back what they had lost, would go to the East Zone and fetch their things from Kleinwanzleben. So she contacted people she knew. Some of them were now at the top of the party – the SED – and had a say in the new administration, and a mention of the name of Horst Heilmann was enough for most doors to open before her. He had been part of the Communist resistance in Berlin, they said, part of the *Rote Kapelle*. He and Schulze-Boysen and Libertas and the rest were feted as heroes in East Germany – later a street was even named after him in Leipzig.

Mother cycled off and slipped across the border – she was almost caught by two Russian soldiers – and all she had with her were the keys to the house and a bag of ground black pepper for self-defence and with them a letter from Horst Heilmann's father:

Halle (Saale) den 4.9.1946

An den
Herrn Landrat des Kreises Wanzleben
in Wanzleben

Frau Hildegard Voll war die Braut meines infolge aktiver Teilnahme an der Widerstandsbewegung Schulze-Bosen am 22.12.1942 hingerichteten Sohnes Horst Heilmann. Frau Voll selbst war mit meinem Sohn Horst und Schulze-Boysen, der der Lehrer der beiden an der Universität war, auch politisch eng verbunden. Frau Voll verdient es infolgedessen bei ihren Bemühungen um Rückführung des inzwischen von der Beschlagnahme frei gegebenen Inventars der Familie Dr. Schneider, nachdrücklichst unterstützt zu werden.

Ich bitte Sie, Frau Voll jede mögliche Unterstützung zuteil werden zu lassen.

Dr. Ing. Adolf Heilmann
Stadtbaurat.[4]

[4] Halle (Saale) 4th September 1946
To: The Prefect
Wanzleben Council
Wanzleben
Frau Hildegard Voll was the wife of my son, Horst Heilmann. My son was executed on 22.12.1942 on grounds of active participation in the Schulze-Boysen resistance movement. Frau Voll was herself also politically closely associated with my son, Horst, and with Schulze-Boysen, who was the couple's teacher at the university. Frau Voll unquestionably deserves, therefore, to be supported in her attempts to retrieve the inventory belonging to Dr Schneider, now no longer subject to confiscation.
I would ask you to provide Frau Voll with every possible assistance.
Dr Adolf Heilmann
Council Building Inspector.

The remainder of her trip to Kleinwanzleben was by bus. She visited Papa Schneider's business connections, Rabbethge and Olbricht, who received her with open arms, putting her up and supporting her in her fight with the local authorities. She was called a spy and a capitalist, and they tried to get rid of her with threats, until a message came through from the most powerful man in Sachsen, Vice-president Robert Siewert. Mother was given the right not only to have their possessions returned but also to travel with them to the West Zone, and a train carriage was placed at her disposal.

The courtyard was empty when Mother returned to the manor. The clock on the tower had stopped at quarter to six – and she could see in her mind's eye the farm's foremen swinging from the trees. They had been lynched when the Russian Army came and liberated the forced labourers – most of them were prisoners of war from Poland and they were quick to get their revenge. Mother let herself in through the front door and tiptoed through the rooms. Everything had been plundered, and she was given an armed escort by the police and went from neighbour to neighbour reclaiming the things they had stolen.

She marched into the Niemüller's. They were in the middle of a meal in their dining room, and she seized everything in the room. Then she visited the former principal and pointed to the grand piano. It was theirs. Their bookcases were scattered far and wide and had been used for anything but books – washing, tableware – and she pulled the rug out from under Papa Schneider's solicitor, who had also been hoarding ill-gotten gains. Mother had the wine dug up from the garden, and she found the silver, the Meissner porcelain and the paintings that had been rolled up and hidden away in the cellar. It was all loaded onto the train and sent to the West. She was profuse in her thanks to the removal men and the party secretary and Olbricht and Siewart and gave them most of the wine and hoped to see them again in happier times!

Once she had had everything sent home to Einbeck and unpacked, Mother brought out the snaps. Now they could celebrate! She distilled her own schnapps using treacle – sugar beet schnapps. It dripped out of the tube and down into a glass flask and still tasted of raw alcohol even though she filtered it through charcoal. Papa Schneider had cheered up – he had his paintings and his books and could clip his fountain pens in his jacket pocket – and Grandmother was out of bed for the first time. Eva put on her best dress, and Inge laughed. They all sat down in their old dining room and then they raised their glasses and said *'Prost!'*, their smiles broad and their mouths black.

Falster lay too far north ever to have a proper summer – and too far south to have a winter. It didn't snow, and the sun didn't shine. It just rained and was grey and cold and foggy, and the wind drove in from the Baltic and swept across the flat fields. It was a comfortless place, and when

December came a Christmas tree stood at the top of the chimney on the Nykøbing Sugar Factory as though thinking of leaping to its death.

The heating was turned right up when Grandmother came to visit at Christmas. The guest room in the cellar was made ready with lace and Schweizerdrops smelling of mint and chocolate, and then we fetched her from the station. We stood freezing on the platform looking for the first sign of the train from Rødby Ferry. It rumbled across Christian IX's bridge and came to a halt with a screech of brakes – Deutscher Bundesbahn – and the doors opened and Grandmother stepped down with fur and hat and gloves and valise. *'Ach, Hildemäuschen!'*, she said and embraced Mother. Father took the suitcase, and I helped her out to the car. On the way home I could already hear the sound of wrapping paper and knew I had been a good boy even before she asked the question – *'Na, bist du auch artig gewesen?'*

Grandmother had brought chocolate and roasted almonds and a new book of poems called *Des Knaben Wunderhorn*. After dinner, when Mother disappeared into the kitchen and Father tidied up, we sat by ourselves in the sitting room to read them aloud. On the first page there was fire crackling in the hearth, and a cat purring, and the scent of pine in the heat. I turned the pages, and it was snowing outside, a post-horn echoed in the distance, and mountain landscapes with castles and knights unrolled under a sky filled with angels. Then the lights were switched on, and Father came in, and the fire and the cat and the tree and the castles and knights were all snuffed out. Father shook his head.

'Look at you sitting there in the pitch dark! You can't see anything!' he said, looking around at the polished mahogany table, the carpets lying without a wrinkle, the silverware. Everything was in place. He nodded and said, *'Schlafengehen'*, and I kissed Grandmother goodnight and went up to bed. The rain dashed against the windows, and I couldn't fall asleep. Christmas was further from Hans Ditlevsensgade 14 than I dared to dream of.

We followed the German Advent calendar, and Grandmother always made sure she was there when I opened the window on 6th December. That was the day St Nicholas handed out presents to children who had behaved, while those who hadn't were beaten by Knecht Ruprecht and shoved into his sack – I had been thinking about it for ages. He would come creeping out of the cupboard at night and sidle over to my bed, birch rod in hand, sack across his shoulder, and would shove his face up close to mine – he had red eyes and a hooked nose – and I hid under the duvet, screwed up my eyes and held my breath until I heard the door close. In the morning a package lay in the shoe I had put out for St Nicholas, and it was all over until next time. Grandmother had put in a good word for me and kept Knecht Ruprecht at bay.

From then on it was just a matter of unwrapping the days, and they were full of the sweets that lay in the shoe outside my door – French nougat, jelly babies, marzipan – and waiting at the end of the line was Christmas Eve. It was hard to make time go fast enough. The rain beat down. It was dark. Grandmother and I played cards in the cellar,

and she always apologized – *'Ach nein, das tut mir so leid'* –
when she took a trick. We sucked Schweizerdrops, which
melted in the heat of the radiator – Father had turned the
heating right up to rule out any risk of a chill or the 'flu –
and in the evenings she read aloud from romantic classics
by E.T.A. Hoffmann – *Nussknacker und Mausekönig* or *Der
goldene Topf* – the gothic lettering in her books was just as
frightening as the stories and looked like magic spells. I was
convinced that Grandmother could make any wish come
true, and what I wished for most was snow.

I leapt out of bed and peered out of the window, but it
was the same every day – there was no break in the greyness
and in the end I stopped believing. Christmas came but it
didn't snow. In the afternoon we went to Klosterkirke – the
bells were chiming, people walking in clusters holding hats
and umbrellas – and I hated walking up the aisle and sitting
in a pew, where everyone moved away, looked elsewhere.
It took an eternity to get through the service. It was for
everyone else and shut us out. And when we folded our
hands together, I prayed that 'Silent Night' would not be
one of the carols this year. After the initial prayer came the
first carol – 'Det kimer nu til julefest' – and then we sang
'Et barn er født i Bethlehem' and 'Julen har bragt velsignet
bud' and I staked my life on a miracle and lost and died
of shame when they finished off with 'Silent Night'. For
Mother sang in German, *'Stille Nacht! Heil'ge Nacht!'* You
could hear it quite clearly, and people shifted in their chairs
and coughed – and in my mind's eye I saw the entire con-
gregation turning and staring and pointing at us, and all I

97

could do was sing along and do my best to drown out her voice in Danish.

What mattered most for Father was that things were neat and tidy, and Christmas Eve was a mess. It was a struggle getting a tree into the living room, and when we got home from church we would lay the table and have a nice time decorating the tree according to fixed rules that involved a minimum of damage and of fire risk. He placed a bucket of water beside the tree, fetched the boxes of Christmas decorations up from the cellar and laid them all out on the bureau, the golden balls one side and the silver ones the other. Then he counted the candle-holders and took the same number of candles out from the stash in the cupboard – there were enough to last for the next hundred years – and hung them on the tree. It was not a Danish Christmas tree full of all sorts of paper decorations and flags and strewn with glitter that – Mother snorted – looked so cheap. The glass balls and the candle-holders hung in ordered rows on our Christmas tree, which was so German that it hurt, and as the crowning glory Father placed a star made of steel at the top.

After Christmas dinner and pudding Father lit the candles in the living room – it was dangerous and made a mess and gave such poor light you couldn't see a thing – and then it was time for presents – *'Bescherung'* – and we were summoned to the Christmas tree.

'Ach! Wie schön!' said Grandmother.

Mother provided accompaniment on her accordion as we stood in a row and sang carols in German and Danish and German again, and admired the tree glittering in the darkness on this one occasion of the year when Father pulled out the plug. Eventually the moment arrived. We had got to the presents, and they were nearly all for me. Mother got cheroots and vodka and a cheque from Father, and Father got a sweater that was the right size and not itchy and was just like the one he had already. I cannot remember what Grandmother was given, but it was all over quickly and we sat there looking at the tree – Mother lit a cheroot and poured herself a vodka. Father fished out the key and opened the lid of the gramophone in the large mahogany radiogram and put on a record with the Wiener Sängerknaben, and we listened to the choir of boys my age singing *'Kling Glöckchen, Klingelingeling'*.

Once the singing died away, the ceremony was over, and Father immediately started putting things back in place and removing any trace of Christmas. He rolled up the ribbons, took down the Advent wreath and everything was carried back down into the cellar. Mother was in the kitchen, and I was left sitting with Grandmother in the living room waiting to see which candle would be the last to go out on the tree. Outside it was dark and the rain was falling again, and Grandmother smiled a secret smile and handed me a parcel that she had been saving.

'Hier, kleines Knüdchen, und fröhliche Weihnachten,' she said.

I ripped off ribbon and paper – it was a glass ball and inside it was a house. It was our house! Then I turned the glass on its head and looked out through the window. And it was snowing.

Papa Schneider started up his businesses again and established himself in the West. He had applied for compensation for his losses in East Germany – '*Entschädigung*' – and they settled in Einbeck. Inge travelled back to Mexico, where her mother was living – she was married to a diplomat – Eva went to domestic science school and dreamed of finding a husband, and Mother was to resume her studies at university. They kept Grandmother company at home, playing cards and reading aloud – she was too ashamed of her looks to set foot out of doors – and when visitors came, she withdrew into her bedroom and waited for them to go.

Papa Schneider had a good reputation and was one of the first Germans to be invited abroad on an official visit. He went to Holland and after that was due to go to Turkey. Just to be on the safe side he had himself operated on for gallstones before he left – he was a very correct man and was representing the country. It was as though he were adjusting a tie in his insides. It was a simple operation, no trickier than tying a Windsor knot, but something or other went wrong.

For the second time Grandmother lost a husband on the operating table, and in 1948, terribly disfigured, she was left among the ruins of her life with two daughters and a corpse. She drew a veil across her face and they went over to the hospital. Auntie Gustchen and the family from Biebrich had already arrived and received them dressed in black, while Papa Schneider lay in the bed as cold and rigid and unapproachable as ever. The same thought was in everyone's mind, but none dared say it, and in the end it was left to Mother to go across and feel whether Papa Schneider really was dead.

She was going to feel the pulse in his neck but didn't dare touch him – his eyes were closed – and she doubted whether a heart ever beat inside him. Mother put her ear to his mouth and listened for his breathing. There was a faint movement of his lips. She pulled back her head but it was too late! He had breathed his last whispering it to her, the name, his secret, and Mother knew what he was called. She stared at Grandmother and the family, who were standing agog in the doorway, waiting, but the word was stuck in her throat. She could say nothing and simply nodded when Auntie Gustchen asked *'Tot?'* Either God had failed to call Papa Schneider to him or else he had lost courage at the last moment, and now it was her turn.

After the funeral Mother picked up the telephone and rang the bank. They had nothing to live off except the contents of Kleinwanzleben. Everything else was in the form of loans or investments that would be withdrawn. She lied and told Grandmother and Eva that state compensation was on its way – then she looked for a job and found work as a mobile rail secretary, which was all there was to be had. Mother learnt touch-typing and banged away at the typewriter in the new high-speed trains – the D trains – criss-crossing a bombed-out Germany at 120 characters a minute. It was hard work. She did not make enough to support them and constantly had to put up with scarcely veiled proposals from male travellers. They became her boss for an hour and could contrive to dictate things for her to type like, 'Can I tempt you to a drink in the buffet car?' or 'You can earn more in a hotel'. Once in a while they became aggressive – she could see it from their glistening faces when they entered the compartment – and she had to get help from the ticket collector. It was most dangerous in stations at night, and before long it happened. There was nothing but a bag of pepper between her and the attacker who pounced on her in Hamburg, and she flung it in his eyes and fled, pursued by his screams.

It was a heaven-sent opportunity when she was con-tacted by Tesdorph and the director, Arnth-Jensen, from the Danish Sugar Factories. Papa Schneider had had connec-tions to Denmark because he grew sugar beet seed and had substantial exports – he was one of the market leaders – and now they wanted to help and invited Mother to Copenha-gen. She was booked into a hotel, and they held a dinner for her at the smart Wivex restaurant – the company's English manager, Rose, was there, too. The following day she saw the little mermaid and the changing of the guard in front of Amalienborg palace and went to Tivoli. The coloured lights twinkled, people laughed, and the peacock's tail fanned out in the Pantomine Theatre – and Pierrot and Harlequin fought over Columbine. Mother looked at the shop-fronts and went up the Round Tower and looked out across the city, and her first impressions were overwhelming. No ruins, no invalids, no hunger – life was in technicolour, and she couldn't believe her eyes.

A week later Arnth-Jensen took her to one side and said that what they could do for her was to offer her a job at the Danish Sugar Factories. Mother accepted gratefully, travelled home and told them first the good news – that she had found a job – and then the bad news – that it was in Denmark. She would have to be away from them for a time but she could send money home every month. The Danes were a friendly people. It was a fairytale country and everything was as small as in Toyland.

It was 1950. The dust had scarcely settled after the war when Mother arrived in Nykøbing on a scooter – a Vespa – frozen stiff and with her scarf flapping in the wind. She had left Einbeck and driven at 60 kph up the motorway – it was late in the year and wet and cold – until she reached Travemünde. She took the ferry and stood on deck watching the mainland disappear and sink into the Baltic with everything she had known and loved and owned – and her route to Falster was so improbable that it ought never to have happened.

Mother woke up in the Seamen's Mission and got herself ready to go to work at the Sugar Factory. She had been employed in the laboratory but had no idea what was awaiting her. For the only trace of sweetness in Nykøbing was in the sugar that they produced. People looked at her sideways and wouldn't reply when she asked a question. Her boss, Hr Møller, became keener and keener to help her, giving her a hand with retorts and Bunsen burners and charts and insisting on accompanying her back to the hotel so that nothing would happen to her – the workers stood at the factory gates whistling after her and laughing and shouting words she didn't understand – and she turned him away at the door. Hr Møller changed his tune, became threatening and said that she should watch her step, and Mother hurried inside. She packed her things, put on her coat and took a hold of her suitcase, and then she sat down on the edge of the bed. She covered her face in her hands, shaking and trembling but unable to cry – it was as though she had no tears left. It was no good. She had to stay.

It was a godforsaken hole and so full of hostility that she had trouble crossing the street. Fru Jensen was one of the few who looked after her. Her husband worked on the Orupgård estate. Mother rented a room in their house – it was small and there was no door, just a curtain that you had to draw aside – and she hardened herself and went to the Sugar Factory and gritted her teeth and bore it. She despised these squat, fat people, called them 'dwarves' in the letters she wrote home every week for as long as Grandmother was alive – and, if anyone had told her that it was here of all places that she would find the love of her life, she would have laughed and shaken her head. Never!

It happened on the Market Square one Sunday, as Father came walking by with two cream pastries in his hand on his way to make one of his usual calls. He was tall and slim and shone like the sun – when I asked Mother why she fell for him, she always replied that he was a handsome man and still had both his arms and legs. Most men of her generation were either dead or invalid – there was no one left in Germany but children and old people – and she determined to make his acquaintance. This was not so easy, for she could not address him on the street – only prostitutes did that kind of thing – and Mother knew no one who could introduce them to each other. Time passed, the mountains of beet in front of the Sugar Factory shrank, and the steam from the chimney thinned to a trickle. The season was coming to an end. She had to return home not knowing what awaited her there or how they would make ends meet. Then the stroke of luck came and their paths crossed.

F ather happened to be on his way to a rehearsal with the male voice choir accompanied by the estate manager from Orupgård, while Mother was taking a walk with Fru Jensen, who knew him. So this was Hildegard Voll, who worked in the laboratory. They were going the same way, and Mother and Father spoke German. He was gentle and polite, and there was no ring on his finger. From now on they could greet each other when they met, and Mother made sure that they met often, and she flirted at the gro-cer's, bumped into him by chance in the park and asked him whether he would invite her along to the company do at the Baltic Hotel.

Mother wrote that she had found the man of her life, and Grandmother was beside herself and burst into tears when she read it – a foreign man in a foreign country, and he wasn't even related to anyone she knew! Mother did not leave at the end of the season. Father invited her back to

Nybrogade for coffee and cream pastries. The place was neat and tidy, and he showed her the pictures he had bought at auction – the country road, the harbour, the bit of forest – and Mother smiled and went across, sat down at the grand piano and flipped the music back to the first page. It was Mozart.

Farmor had worked herself to death and died of arthritis long since, but you could still hear her walking, her stick tapping in the grandfather clock down in the living room – tick-tock, tick-tock. The pains had got worse and worse until she couldn't move anymore and, when Carl was buried, she lay down in her bed and never got up again. Father came by and gave her hot compresses and cold compresses – nothing helped. The doctors had no remedy for arthritis and did not know what caused it – the latest theory was that it came from your teeth – and she was told that her only hope lay in experimental treatment.

They pulled all Karen's teeth out one by one. Her smile disappeared and was replaced by a false one that she could put in her mouth. So she smiled and she smiled while bone and gristle were seared with pain and joints twisted – her hands looked like claws – and, when Father introduced Mother to her and told her that they were to be married, he couldn't tell whether she was happy for them or whether it was just the false teeth. They met just that once. Mother asked how she was, and Karen smiled and nodded and didn't understand a word she said – either in German or English. There was nothing they could say to each other. Mother tried out her Danish, and then the door opened and in came Leif – Father's older brother, who limped – with Kamma, his fat wife, and their three children. They paid their respects, aloof and cold, as the children shouted and leapt about, and when they ran towards the bed Father shouted 'Careful!' He took Mother's hand and said goodbye and they left it at that for the time being. Within a couple of days Farmor had taken her false teeth out.

Karen was laid in an urn next to Grandfather. I never got to know her but I missed her, and I sat waiting on the floor in front of the grandfather clock, where she walked again. It had come from her parents' farm, Klovergården in Sildestrup, and every time the hour struck I ran and opened the front door hoping that Farmor would be standing in the street outside. Of course she wasn't, but I had a sense that she was on her way, that she was nearing the house – tick-tock, tick-tock – and that before long she would have caught up with time and would ring the doorbell and say hello.

The school test decided whether you were ready to start in the first year – parents lined the walls of the room watching. I sat at a desk among the other children and looked across at Mother, who beamed and was happy, waving to me. We were given a pencil and a piece of paper with a house and a flagpole, and Miss Kronov, the teacher, gave us our task, which was to draw a flag that pointed downwind – the wind direction was shown by an arrow. I didn't pass. There was nothing wrong with the wind direction, but I had drawn the German flag, and Mother apologized and it was agreed that it would be best if I waited a year.

Mother laughed and sang revolution all the whole way home – *'Pulver ist Schwarz, Blut ist rot, Golden flackert die Flamme!'* – and soon afterwards we went down to stay with Grandmother in Frankfurt, and she put me in a German kindergarten class. We walked up Kettenhofweg in the morning – I had been given a knapsack – and crossed Mendelsohnsstraße, where the tram ran, with the baker and the paper shop on the corner, and a little further down the street Mother handed me over in a doorway to a woman with a dark dress and a bun. I was in shock when she fetched me again in the afternoon. The school was ruled with a rod of iron and I refused to return, digging my heels in until in the end Mother sighed and surrendered and bought a year's subscription to the botanical gardens, the Palmengarten, and taught me herself.

We read in the mornings – *Winnetou* and *Kleiner Muck* and *Max und Moritz* – and drew and chose to skip maths and go to the natural history museum and look at dinosaurs instead. It was a couple of streets away and was called the Senckenberg Museum, and I loved it. It was a castle built in the baroque style with broad steps, double doors, tall windows, mirrors and gilded stucco. The skeletons were gigantic. They looked as though they were walking round the room or crouching with jaws wide open – as if the dawn of primeval time was about to break.

There was Tyrannosaurus and Brachiosaurus – and a raptor that had wings and could fly. On the first floor there were stuffed animals – giraffes and elephants, fish and fowl and mammals watching us from behind the glass. At the very top there were fossils and stones, and Mother held my hand when we got to the Egyptian mummies. We trudged through skulls and human skeletons along the earth's longest story, which lasted four billion years and ended in an ice cream.

After we had eaten lunch I was let off and was free to do what I wanted, and what I wanted was to go the Palmengarten. Just up Beethovenstraße, past the church ruins and over Bockenheimer Landstraße you stood at the entrance to another world. There was an explosion of flowers as I walked through the turnstile, and the beds in front of the huge white Tropicarium shone in a thousand colours. There were refreshments on the verandah, where people sat drinking coffee and eating cakes. If you turned right, you came to the botanical gardens and the greenhouses, and I ran off left down to the lake and the boat hire. I rowed on the lake for hour after hour and spent all my pocket money, and when I didn't have any more 50 Pfennig pieces – that was what it cost – I stepped ashore and travelled across the steppes and on from one continent to the next, playing the explorer. There was dry and stony, there was sandy with cacti – and there was humid and thick with orchids. The tropical heat slapped you across the face in the palm house, where the glass roof rose in domes above a jungle full of steep-sided grottos and waterfalls. Fantastic butterflies floated between the palms, and the air was alive with the chirrup of birds I had never heard before, and I forced my way through leaves and lianas lured on by an Incan treasure.

It was almost impossible to get me out of Palmengarten when evening fell and Mother came to fetch me from the playground where I would be sitting in the climbing frame. It was shaped like an aeroplane, and I sat up front at the controls and was flying to America. It was a long way across the Atlantic. It grew darker and darker, and the playground had long since emptied. Mother stood there freezing and begging me to come down until in the end she succeeded by dangling the prospect of sweets at the exit, but it was closed when we got there. The following day she was ill, was running a temperature, and was sent to hospital. I visited her with Grandmother, and we were told that she had pneumonia and was close to dying. It was terrible. Father came down from Nykøbing to look after us, and I just waited to be given my punishment.

The bedroom at Grandmother's looked out on a yard with garages and a large chestnut tree, where there was an Alsatian that was always barking. This was Pension Gölz. Frau Gölz was a Jew. She was large and fat and wore dresses with large flowery patterns. She sat in her armchair in an over-furnished sitting room where she had her sofa bed, and she rented out the rest of the house. It was the Djugaric family who were in charge of running the place – they came from Yugoslavia – and Frau Djugaric washed and cleaned in slippers and apron. Her husband was the caretaker and their daughter had auburn hair and was called Dolores.

'Wie im film,' she said. *'Dolores.'*

And, as in the film, I fell in love with her on the spot even though she was older than I was. Most of the time she would sit making herself up. She had lifted the mirror on her dressing table and the drawer below was crammed with make-up. And then we listened to records, Beatles and Rolling Stones – 'Paint it black', 'We love you' – and a mysterious track called 'The road to Cairo'. They had television, and I liked nothing better than to visit them and stay to dinner. Her father made *chevapcechi* – small rolls of mince with chopped onion and garlic and pepper – and when he fried them in the kitchen the whole house smelt of oil and onions. The food was dished up with bread and tomato sauce. Then the television was turned on and the adverts rolled across the screen – for building societies and washing powder and cigarettes. *'Wer wird denn gleich in die Luft gehen? Greife lieber zur HB'*, and Afri-Cola, *'sexy-mini-super-flower-pop-op-cola'* – interrupted between times by cartoons, *Die Mainzelmännchen* and *Onkel Otto*. Then came the theme tune and on came *The Avengers*, in which John Steed saved the world from robots, assisted in the nick of time by his partner in leather, Emma Peel. I felt like a double agent when I crept through the glass door at Grandmother's – it shivered – and kissed her and Mother goodnight, for my secret mission was to see as much television as possible without being discovered.

I went round as soon as I could and asked to see Dolores. We took jay rides on the tram into the centre and strolled up and down the pedestrian precinct and in the Kaufhof. Once in a while we went to Palmengarten and rowed on the lake, and I fished coins up for her from the wishing well in the garden – 1, 2, 5, 10 and 20 Pfennigs in copper, 50 Pfennigs and 1 and 2 Deutschmarks in silver, and she showed me how to stick my hand up the vending machine and get a Coca-Cola out. So when I was told that we were going home to Nykøbing, both my flames were put out, Dolores and Emma Peel, and I sat in the yard stripping the green off chestnut leaves and waiting for Dolores to ask her if she would come and visit us in Denmark, and she said she would.

Mother took me with her to Café Krantzler on the Hauptwache, and we ate cakes, and she said that we were to go to the opera that evening, and that was to be our farewell to Frankfurt. It lay in ruins on the Opernplatz – huge and hollow and burnt out – and I had to wear a suit and have my hair brushed for an hour, and Grandmother washed my face with her spit and a handkerchief. Mother smelled of perfume and was dazzling in her jewels and furs, and this was how we accompanied each other to the opera to hear *Die Meistersänger*. It was Wagner, she said, as we settled into our seats in the auditorium. The chandeliers glittered and there was a buzz of people. We were in the new theatre on Theaterplatz, and it was nothing like I had imagined, until the music began and the curtain rose – there were broken columns and smoke and rubble on the stage.

Mother explained the plot, told me what was happening, whispering and chattering and telling me about the time she had heard Richard Strauss in Berlin in 1940, when Hitler came into the concert hall with Strauss's widow, Pauline, at his side. Everyone had risen to their feet, and even though she had been frightened, Mother had remained seated with Horst and Harro and Libertas. I'd never have got up either, I said, nodding and sinking deeper and deeper into my seat until I fell asleep to music that went on forever. The shadows flickered, the sirens howled, and all around us flames engulfed the opera and razed it to the ground.

My first day at school was just like Christmas and New Year and all my birthdays rolled into one. Grandmother had come up to Nykøbing to celebrate it. She had brought with her a '*Wundertüte*', a colourful paper cone full of goodies that children were given in Germany to mark the day. I had never in my life seen so many sweets – it was almost too heavy to carry. And now we were ready, and Father took a photograph of me in the front door, Mother went with me to school, dropped me off at the entrance, said goodbye and gave me a kiss on the cheek. I was looking forward to it and ran into the playground, where children and teachers were chatting and laughing, paying no attention to me, and I felt rather lost until first one and then another caught sight of me and before I knew it I was standing at the centre of the whole crowd clutching my cone of sweeties – and dressed in short *Lederhosen* and green knee-length stockings – and then they started up, slowly and rhythmically the whole school struck up in unison the chorus I was to hear for the rest of the day, for years to come, for the rest of my life: 'Ger-man pig! Ger-man pig! Ger-man pig!'

Nykøbing Falster is a town that is so small that its beginning is its end. If you are in it, you cannot get out – and if you are outside, you cannot get in. You pass right through it, and the only trace the town leaves is on your clothes – the smell of manure in summer and sugar beet in winter. This is where I was born in 1960, and it was the nearest I could come to not being at all.

Our house was on Hans Ditlevsensgade 14, in the last terrace before the fields of beet and Vesterskoven woods. It was the image of a red-brick house with a hedge and a garage and a garden gate, but it wasn't that. It was a nightmare from which there was no escape. The front door was always locked, and so was the door to the cellar, and Father had the keys in his pocket. The curtains were drawn, and the windows looked inwards, closing around each other and our family, which consisted of Mother and Father and me – and no one else but us.

It was the three of us around the dining table at breakfast, lunch and dinner year in, year out. When Christmas came we stretched out our arms but couldn't make a ring around the tree, and at New Year we sat, the three of us, and drank champagne, blew paper streamers and drank each other's health when the clock struck twelve. We celebrated by ourselves, our birthdays, Easter, Whitsun, and at midsummer we watched the bonfires from a distance, listening to them all singing 'Our homeland we love … ' And every single summer holiday it was the three of us, Mother and Father and me, for always.

We went touring by car to Bøtø and Corselitz and drove up to Pomlenakke and walked among the beeches on the ridge, and Mother and I looked for flat stones along the sea shore and played ducks and drakes. Father raked through the beach with his walking stick and fell into a daydream counting the grains of sand. In the autumn we hunted for mushrooms in the woods, and Father beat on the woodpiles with his stick. Some of them gave out notes and you could play a tune on them. In the spring we would pick anemones and lilies-of-the-valley. Mother put them on the table in little figureens of Royal Danish porcelain – a girl with a basket and a fisherman – and we ate our dinner and time went round in circles of sameness.

The dining room was filled with Papa Schneider's furniture, shiny, dark, mahogany – the chairs we sat on, the table, the sideboard. It was his cutlery we ate with, his monogram engraved in the silver, and when knife and fork lay at each side of your plate they spelt out SS. It was his tableware – Villeroy & Boch for everyday and for special occasions his Meissner porcelain. It had flower patterns in clear colours, and when Mother said *'das Meissner'* and brought it out, the words chimed like Christmas and New Year. It was stacked away with pink tissue paper between each plate – enough for five courses for twelve people and bowls and tureens – and to use it was a sacred act. An embroidered white tablecloth was spread on the table. There was cut glass, and beside our places lay napkin rings like handcuffs made of silver. We sat down and followed the ritual, saying the same things, doing the same things, and the cutlery would clink and play glockenspiel tunes on the porcelain about the fear of falling to pieces.

We lived alone, and there was no place for the world around us. Mother and Father had no friends or acquaintances and no social life. Where my grandparents should have been there was no one – and that went for my Danish cousins and uncles and aunts, too. It was strange not being related to anyone. Father never spoke about it, and if I asked about them I was told that all that was a closed chapter, as though that explained everything. Mother could go so far as to say that Grandfather had been a dreamer and had squandered everything, to which Father replied that it had been tough. They never went into more detail, but I kept on at them, until one evening Father stopped beating round the bush and told it to me straight. They had cut us off, washed their hands of us – and in my mind's eye I could see the blood and our severed limbs strewn around the living room and could not understand how they could be so heartless.

Ib had disappeared immediately after the occupation, and Father did not hear from his younger brother again until 1944, when the telephone rang. He had joined the resistance movement, and Father knew that it was him when riots broke out in Odense and sabotage spread. You could chart his movements across the country from one place to another each time something was blown up – a railway or the factory owned by a collaborator. Ib had always made trouble and now he could do what he wanted – until at last he had to go underground. He had to go to Sweden, but couldn't take his girlfriend, Jeanne, with him unless he married her – and he wanted to borrow Father's dark suit for the wedding – if that was ok?

It was not up Father's street at all – and Ib may have been wanting to tease him – but he went to Copenhagen anyway, because he was to be best man. Holding the suit up in front of him on a coat-hanger, he walked out to Frederiksberg, where Ib lived, but there was no one home. He had taken an address under a fake name somewhere else. Father continued from one flat to the next – Vesterbro, Østerbro, Christianshavn – asking for Andersen or Nielsen or whatever other name Ib went by – and he unravelled the clues until he rang the bell on the right door and was hauled inside.

Ib's eyes were swollen and clotted with blood and he had been badly beaten up. He sat down in front of Father in the kitchen, lit a cigarette and gave him a lop-sided smile.

'Thanks a lot!' he said. 'You've been a great help. You've just shown the Germans the way to this safe house and put an end to one of our cells. What the hell do you think you're doing?!'

Then he got to his feet saying that there was no time to lose, and Father went with him to the house of one of the men who was to ferry Ib and Jeanne to Sweden. She was waiting there with the priest, and in no time they were married and jumped into the back of a van, Ib shouting that he'd make sure Father got it back – the suit – and then they drove off safely.

Things were getting too hot for Ib. He had been picked up a few weeks earlier and the Gestapo had interrogated him. He had cigarette burns up his arms, but he had said nothing and played the innocent. He had been transferred to an ordinary prison, where he had been sprung by resistance people – not so much to save his life as to stop him talking, for he knew too much. Ib returned in 1945 with the Danish Brigade, cursing the Swedes, who were traitors and had cooperated with the occupying forces. But most of all he nurtured a vicious and savage hatred for Germans that simmered beneath the surface ready to erupt – and next time it was Father's turn to be married, and his bride was that beautiful girl from Germany.

They made their excuses. They couldn't come, Ib and Leif and Annelise – not even Auntie Petra. None of them wanted to come to the wedding. Mother said that they could manage without them, and Father bought a new suit. Then they travelled down to Kelkheim in the Taunus mountains, where Auntie Eva lived with Helmut, her husband. For she had found one at last. He was small and round and of good stock, and they were the only people present at the town hall aside from Grandmother. After coffee and cakes they were married in an empty church – a quick kiss with pursed lips – and Helmut drove them to Königstein, where they were to spend the night at a smart hotel set in the middle of a park called Sonnenhof. In the evening they all went to the restaurant – Haus der Länder – and Father kept the bill as a memento of the day. They had *paté de foie* and toast *mit Butter* (4 Deutschmarks), turtle soup (7 Deutschmarks), Chateaubriand steak with *pommes frites* and *sauce béarnaise* and salad (12 Deutschmarks), and for dessert there was sorbet. At half-past eleven the wedding was over, and it had come to 135 Deutschmarks in all, including beverages.

Now Mother's name was Romer Jørgensen – Hildegard Lydia Voll Romer Jørgensen, and that was the first thing they took away from her. She was not allowed to be called Romer, and Father could do nothing about it. A veto had been granted on the use of the name. She hung her bridal bouquet to dry and put it away for safe keeping. And she used the name anyway, even though it was not in her passport. It was German, and so was she – and she would not be allowed to forget it. The Second World War had never ended as far as Mother and Father and our family went. Nykøbing was still in the grip of the enemy.

She returned to the Sugar Factory for the following season and continued in the laboratory, handing her wages over to Father as people did in those days. He gave her housekeeping money, 25 crowns a week. It didn't go very far, and everything cost over the odds for Mother, saddled with war guilt and paying the price over and over again as she laid the table on the balcony on Nybrogade. She served up lobster bisque and steak and Riesling and melon and cream cakes for Father – he was thin as a rake, she said, and kissed him on the cheek – and for his birthday she gave him a scarf, genuine cashmere. Father had hit lucky, and when he told them about it at choir practice, they couldn't believe their ears and complained to their wives. Why couldn't they make their money go as far as she could and dish up something other than stewed cabbage?

Mother had sold one of the paintings from Kleinwanzleben without telling anyone and had opened a secret account in Germany with her share – Eva and Grandmother got theirs – and she used it to make their lives a little sweeter and to help fight her corner. For she did hit back and was subjected to a campaign of spite, as gossip went the rounds – and things were not made easier by the fact that she was responsible for analysing the sugar percentages in the laboratory. This was what determined what the farmers got for their beet, and they complained, saying the figures were too low, but she refused to alter them by a fraction. Even the management was out to get her, since she had been employed over their heads by the company director, Arnth-Jensen.

It was difficult to say who hated her most, and she made it all that much worse by being lah-di-dah, as they put it. When the time came for the big summer outing with the Brage choir, where they all took their families and had lunch in the village of Virket, Mother was not invited and Father resigned. He made a good second tenor and could play the trombone – he had been in the Boy Scouts brass band – but the only thing I ever heard him play was a record, a lacquer master, with the Brage male voice choir singing 'How fresh and green the woodland glades'. He always put it on at New Year – we would sit in the sitting room and light the Christmas tree for the last time – and when it was over and you asked him what he wanted to listen to now, Father would reply that he did not care for music.

She was the perfect wife, he said at the lodge meetings when they broached the subject – the German problem – and he shuffled back home in his evening clothes as though he was returning from a funeral. Mother questioned him about what went on at the freemasons, and he was ashamed and wouldn't reply, changing instead into other clothes and hitting his top-hat to make it collapse and go flat. He told her later in the evening – of course – and tried to explain, turning their words this way and that, but it only got worse and worse. It was the freemasons or Mother – and Father never wore the hat again.

From then on one thing led to another. He packed his things and chucked in the home guard and he stopped going to the photographic society. This had been his great passion, and the desk was full of hundreds of photographs, where a country road rounded a bend, the oat fields were yellow, the farmsteads idyllic, the views glorious, the cliffs at Møn and Ålholm Castle. They looked like postcards, and there were no people in them – and as time went on people slid out of the picture in reality, too. Father invited guests to dinner, and Mother served up '*Sülzkoteletten*' – complete with the intricate decorations that she cut out in pickled cucumbers and carrots – and people piled their plates high and drank and sang along when she sat at the grand piano and played – but no one invited them back. Their circle narrowed – even childhood friends fell away, until there was no one who wanted to see them – and Mother shrugged her shoulders and despised them and called them proletarians.

It came as a shock to him when Mother told him that he should resign from Danish Building Assurance – it was the last thing Father had to cling on to – and he broke down. He never wept on any other occasion, not once, and it sounded so strange, so distant and hollow. Mother comforted him and explained that he was the mainstay of the company, but still he was no more than … an assistant manager? Henry Mayland had married into his position and was useless. He sat and twiddled his thumbs in his big office because he was Damgård's son-in-law, and he let Father run the business – and he was the one who ought to be the manager.

Father resigned – he always did as she told him – and with some reluctance set off to Copenhagen, made contact with Ib and was employed in his company. He had an advertising agency and swindled, boasted and drank as much as he always had. They had just netted I G Farben, he said with a guffaw, and were bleeding the German swine – and it was all loudmouths and hot air! Mother said he should just put up with it and wait and see what happened. A month passed. Six months. And then the telephone rang at last. It was Victor Larsen, the solicitor. He was on the board of

Danish Building Assurance. Damgård had died, and they wanted to reinstate Father. He was prepared to say yes to anything, but Mother stood firm and forced him to demand what was his by right. There could be no question of him coming out of the meeting as anything other than manager. And Father could hardly believe it himself. He was walking on air as he came in through the front door. He had been made manager! Sub-manager!

Father never managed to achieve proper recognition in the insurance company where he worked for forty-nine years and eight months. He had to learn to live with playing second fiddle to Henry Mayland, who never lifted a finger, and with kissing his wife's hand – Mother couldn't stand her. Father was granted a new title and a new office – a pokey room on the ground floor, from which a staircase led up to the spacious rooms where Mayland occupied a leather chair behind a vast writing desk. After his appointment and the board meeting there was a dinner. Mother had dressed for the occasion, had put up her hair and was as stunning as a film star. He got quite a shock – and she put Fru Mayland in the shade and showed the board of directors from Copenhagen who was the manager's wife around here. Father straightened up, growing taller and taller – and touched seventh heaven when she told him they were to have a child.

They had to find a larger place to live, and the increase in his salary would allow them to buy a house. Mother persuaded him to demand a company car suitable for a manager, and it was to be a Mercedes. He was given the smallest model – a dark-blue Mercedes 180 – and it was the only one of its kind in town. Father gave her a fur coat, an ocelot, and she handed in her notice at the Sugar Factory and sat beside Father in the car. Then he cruised off in first gear, changed into second and took a drive around Nykøbing. It was the last time they saw anyone. From then on the space around them became completely void.

In 1959 they moved into a detached red-brick house on Hans Ditlevsensgade, and Mother had her belongings fetched from Einbeck. They arrived in a goods carriage, were unloaded at the station and ferried home. Then they reinstated the dining room rescued from Kleinwanzleben – sideboard, table and chairs, silver and tableware, all found a place. They unpacked the porcelain, and the double bed and the wardrobes were carried up into the bedroom. They unrolled the carpets in the sitting room, and Mother hung the paintings. Finally, to top it all, they opened one of the bottles of wine left over from Papa Schneider's cellar – it was an 1892 vintage and very expensive – and Father took a taste and said 'Arghhh!', and Mother laughed. It tasted of vinegar. It couldn't travel and had gone off. She saw in her mind's eye the party elite in East Germany, who had been given the wine as a bribe, pouring it out, clinking glasses and screwing up their mouths. She brought out the duvet covers, embroidered with their coat of arms, and made the bed. Father took a look outside, checked everything, locked the front door and lay down to sleep beside my mother, who was a dream in a bed in another country.

Sunlight fell between the curtains in the morning, crept across the floor like a tiger and licked me on the cheek. I always woke before I got eaten. It was gone but I could hear it outside roaring. I was convinced that lions and tigers walked the streets – sometimes there was the sound of other animals too, apes or parrots – and the hedge around our house was there to keep out wild beasts, just like in *Peter and the Wolf*.

What I could hear was the Zoo. I had dreamt about it ever since our teacher, Fru Kronov, had said that we were going on a school outing. We lined up in two rows and marched through the town, past the railway station and on out to Sønder Kohave Wood, and there we walked around Nykøbing Folkepark. There was a kiosk at the entrance, where they sold spaghetti for the monkeys and ice cream for the children.

You could pat the goats, but the he-goats butted with their horns and we ran outside. To the left lay the bears' grotto, where a brown bear danced for sugar lumps and turned round and round in endless circles. Antelopes walked the ploughed fields among the cows, and the flamingos stood on stalks in the lake and rotted from the feet up. The monkeys chewed the bars and made faces and reached out their arms for the spaghetti. The lions were skeletal, their manes moulting, and the giant turtle lay on its back, dead. The stench was awful. At the exit a parrot, a blue and gold macaw, sat rocking from side to side pecking at itself and staring at me with evil yellow eyes, and I could not get it out of my head.

We marched back to the school as though nothing had happened, and behind us the animals howled and bellowed and gathered themselves into a single ear-splitting scream. But no one heard it in Nykøbing. I took a porcelain figure home with me that I had bought at the kiosk with my sweet money. It was a sea lion, and Mother kissed me, gave me a cuddle and put it on the bedside table. There it stood, a memento of my school outing, a souvenir of hell on earth.

Two or three times a year Mother and Father went on major shopping expeditions. We would take the ferry, and the tables juddered as we left the quayside, and King Frederik and Queen Ingrid and Princess Margrethe trembled in their frames on the wall. The woman's voice in the loudspeakers wished us a good crossing in three languages, and for 45 minutes there were no limits to the tax-free shopping. Then it was on to Lübeck, and we walked up through the pedestrian precinct, in and out of the shops. I tried on a jazzy shirt that Mother had found, and dreaded the idea of wearing it to school. We had lunch in the Rathauskeller – *'Wienerschnitzel mit pommes frites'* – and later we went to Niederegger, the confectioner where they made marzipan. I had an Italian ice cream. Mother drank coffee and smoked cheroots.

'Such a marzipan they do not have in Dänemark,' she said, sitting with the shopping bags at her feet – gloves, shoes and

a dress from Jaeger – and Father said how right she was, and nor could you get decent sausages or proper chocolate back home, and then we drove out to the end of the rainbow, where everything you wanted was brought together in one place, Citti Grossmarkt.

It was a cathedral. Even the shopping trolleys were so big that it took two people to push them. We walked along the shelves in the aisles, and everything looked as though you were seeing it through a magnifying glass. There were giant cucumbers and pickled gerkins and more varieties of chips than I had ever seen, and the rows of coloured Smarties went on forever. Father filled up the boot of the car with hams and *sauerkraut* and sausages in tins, with marmalade and salted crackers and chocolate, with wine and vodka. The car was so weighted down on the way home that the traffic in the opposite lane hooted and flashed at us, blinded by our headlights. When we got home, he systematically unpacked all the things we had bought in the sitting room, laying them out and taking a photograph of our haul. Then he stashed them away in the larder down in the cellar, wrote everything down in his diary and registered it all with the price and quantity. Maggi, Dr Oetker, Nutella. We ate frankfurters in the kitchen. Mother served them up with mustard and beetroot. '*Mmmm,*' she said, and Father nodded and speared another sausage from the saucepan. It was as though they were stocking up for the war that was to come – and in a way they were.

Aunt Annelise, my father's sister, was the illegitimate daughter of King Christian IX and called herself Princess Ann. When she went down to collect her invalid pension it was her royal appanage. She was mad as a hatter, and I only knew her because I had been unlucky enough to answer the telephone a few times when she had been on the other end.

'Hello, Knud,' she might say. 'Do you think I might have a word with your father?'

I'd quickly fetch Father, who took the receiver and spoke with her – Mother and I were all ears – and the conversation always ended with Father saying goodbye and 'I'll be sending you a little envelope'. As soon as he put the phone down, it was as though nothing had happened. But it had, and one day the bell rang, and Annelise stood there in the doorway.

I couldn't believe that it was her, Aunt Annelise, sitting in front of me on the sofa smoking one cigarette after the other. Her hands shook, and she had to get a grip on herself to hit the ashtray that Father had set beside her. I was frightened out of my wits, convinced that it was infectious and that soon we would all go mad. Mother came in with a beer – she placed a silver coaster under the bottle so it didn't mark the mahogany – and Annelise said thank you and gabbled in a nervous stream, skating dangerously along the edge of song and dance and swearing and gobbledegook.

Mother and Father whispered together in the kitchen about her afterwards – I wasn't supposed to hear – and when Father said, 'Not on your life!' Mother answered that she had nowhere to go and hadn't even got any clothes. Annelise had been arrested at the English customs smuggling pornography into the country – she had met a man in Nyhavn and they were lovers – the embassy had sent her straight back to Oringe Hospital, but instead she was now on her way to Copenhagen. When it came down to it, she was after money as usual. If Father could just give her a bit, she would vanish as quickly as she had come – and Father gave in and let her stay the night in the guest room.

Never had I heard so many illicit acts referred to at one time. I could hardly believe my ears and dared not think about Aunt Annelise lying and sleeping down in our cellar. When she emerged the following morning, Father handed her an envelope, and she was given some clothes by Mother along with a discarded fur. After savouring her own reflection in the wardrobe mirror, she looked at us as though she expected us to fall on one knee – and then she was out across the ploughed fields, taking the shortest route to Copenhagen, shaking her fist and shouting, 'This place stinks of death and decay!'

Aunt Annelise had been spoilt from the day she opened her eyes on the world. She was the only girl, the youngest, and every day was her birthday. She was pretty and she always had her way, toying with people as though they were her dolls, and they did as she said and played along with her. As she entered her teens, she behaved more and more outrageously. She read novelettes and wanted to be an actress, and she went to dance classes at Birgitte Reimer's, flirting with her husband even though he was old and married with children of her age. One day she would be a film star on her way to Hollywood, the next she would be a nun and renounce everything. When the royal yacht came by and anchored in Nykøbing, she was knocked sideways – rumours were going around about King Christian having affairs in the town – and after that for weeks she was a lady-in-waiting and impossible to talk to. She was a cut above this world, and when she came home with notes from school, Grandfather said that Annelise just had too much imagination.

Annelise lived in a dream, longing for life in the big city, and her great love was amateur dramatics. She lived and breathed for the performances at the Baltic Hotel. On stage she became herself, spreading her wings in the tension of high drama, was Desdemona, was Nora, and could not come down to earth again. She would go partying after the performances and began drinking and going with men, and before her eighteenth birthday she was pregnant. The man was a photographer, Lars Krusell – he had taken pictures of her. They were married by special licence, and Annelise got away from Nykøbing.

They moved to Haderslev and had a daughter, Pernille, but nothing was as she had imagined it would be. There was no part for her to play. Life didn't revolve round her – she boiled nappies and cooked meals – and every day Annelise died a little in normal life. She started hanging out in bars again and met a doctor from northern Zealand, Jørn-Erik, whom she seduced and later married. He was far older than she and agreed to get a divorce. She also was divorced and took Pernille with her – and now the good life started rolling in Copenhagen with theatres, dinners and dancing. She drank cocktails, smoked with a cigarette-holder, and Jørn-Erik wrote prescriptions and supplied her with the substances her dreams were made of – sedatives and morphine. She was a star, she was part of a film, and her success story knew no end.

As a rule Annelise was foul-tempered and depressed – but emerged transformed after every visit to the bathroom. She wore theatre make-up and dressed in dramatic costumes made of satin with sequins and feathers that swirled around her. When she walked down Bredgade with her daughter, people turned to stare, and Pernille hunched up her shoulders and fixed her eyes on the ground. When they reached the square in front of the royal residence at Amalienborg Castle, Annelise would stop and point at the palace saying, 'You see! There it is!' Then she walked up to the gate and rang the bell. They waited and waited, until finally a man opened the door and asked how he could be of assistance. Annelise measured him with her eyes from head to foot and asked what ever he was thinking of. Didn't he know who she was? Princess Ann! He slammed the door shut, and they went on their way – and some weeks later they would be standing there again.

Jørn-Erik could do nothing about it. He was just as hooked on her as she was on medicine. He was a weak, pallid fellow, and she satisfied all his desires as long as he provided her with pills and eggnogs and money to buy clothes and shoes and to hold court – her acquaintances all came to call and played along and laughed at her and continued knocking back the drink. She had another child – a son, Klaus – and never looked after him. It was all chaos. The flat was piled high with mess, the washing-up was never done, they never had meals or clean clothes, Pernille didn't go to school, and one day Jørn-Erik had had enough. He had come home to find all their furniture thrown out of the window of the third floor and strewn across the street with people crowded round. He let himself in, and Annelise gabbled at him, shouting that he had to go down on his knees, and so he fell on his knees and begged her to stop and come to her senses, but she just grew even more furious, and from now on would only be addressed with her royal title.

It was high time Jørn-Erik pulled himself together and did something about it – even though he was worried they might take a look at his prescriptions – and he told Annelise that they were invited to a ball in Corselitze, which the royals visited every summer. She decked herself out in long dress and jewellery and put her hair up, complaining about the car – it was a Volvo and not suitable for her standing – and spent the entire journey talking about the Lord Chamberlain and about the latest gossip from ladies-in-waiting and hairdressers and about affairs in high places. At Vordingborg he turned off the main road and drove towards Marienberg. At the end of the avenue stood some large white-painted buildings. Annelise touched up her make-up in the mirror and prepared for her grand entrance – her eyes were shining and she was lit up for a party – and so they entered Oringe Mental Hospital side by side.

The mental hospital was Vordingborg's largest employer, and that said everything about the place. But if Jørn-Erik thought that he could get rid of Annelise that easily he had another think coming. She had grown up on the other side of the bridge a few kilometres south. She knew people like she knew the back of her hand and immediately picked up what was going on. She exchanged looks with the nurses and the doctor who was filling in the forms: 'Application for the admission of a mentally ill patient'. Once he had completed the forms, he looked up and winked at Jørn-Erik before passing the papers across to Annelise, who was to sign them. And so she did. And then it was Jørn-Erik's turn. He smiled and lowered the pen and started. Something was wrong! This was impossible – they had written the wrong name, it wasn't Annelise who was due to be admitted but he, Jørn-Erik Mølby! He threw down the pen, shook his head and asked what on earth was going on. He wasn't the one who was ill, it was she – he pointed at Annelise and got up – he was a doctor, he should know what he was talking about! Annelise sighed as though she had heard this hundreds of time before, and the doctor sent her an understanding nod. He said that it would, of course, require the signature of the chief of police for him to be forcibly committed using the pink forms but that could be taken care of by a telephone call – and was her husband a danger to himself or to others?

It was Pernille who told me – she was a thin girl with slides in her hair and timid as a mouse. We were at the funeral in Herlev and were standing on our own outside the church, while round us the family was divided into groups, all ignoring each other. Most of them I hadn't seen before and only knew by hearsay, so it was as though they didn't exist in reality. Aunt Annelise was in mourning dress with black veil, black hat, black gloves. She was sobbing like a thing possessed. Jørn-Erik, pale and broken by grief, crossed to talk to Hanne and Jens – he was a commodore in the navy and Pernille had been taken into care by their family. And then Uncle Ib joined the company and gave me a wave – he had developed a beer-belly – and at that point Mother came rushing over, took me by the hand and said that we had better be leaving now, and we drove back to Falster; the atmosphere in the car you could cut with a knife.

Jørn-Erik had been under Annelise's thumb ever since the trip to Vordingborg – how she avoided being certified was still a mystery. She threatened to take the children away if he didn't come to heel and waved the hospital forms and laughed. And Jørn-Erik resigned himself and did as she asked and consoled himself with morphine and booze. He more or less became her slave, said Mother with a shake of her head, and Father said, 'Enough of that now ...' and turned on the car radio – only to switch it off again because it was music. We tried to avoid thinking about it but that was, of course, impossible.

It had gone on for years, until finally Annelise lost interest and went along with a separation provided she was guaranteed a substantial allowance. She kept the youngest, Klaus. Jørn-Erik moved out. Pernille was taken into care at the commodore's – and after a while Jørn-Erik could come and go there as he pleased. He would make drinks before dinner and kept the commodore's wife, Hanne, warm when her husband was away on naval exercises. They celebrated Christmas together and spent holidays together at a derelict farmhouse and kept the threesome going until the telephone rang and it all blew up in their faces. It was the police. They wished to inform him that his son, Klaus Mølby, was dead. He had been found hanging from the kitchen door at the home of Jørn-Erik's former wife, Annelise Romer Jørgensen, and everything pointed to it having been suicide. There were, however, a number of circumstances that they wished to speak to him about. For example, a large quantity of morphine and Valium and amphetamines had been found in the flat along with prescriptions made out in his name – and was he acquainted with someone called ... Princess Ann?

We lived in a house under siege, and Father took no chances at New Year, when things got particularly bad. Children were always ringing the doorbell, throwing bangers and squibs through the letterbox and running away. They nicked the garden gate, overturned the rubbish bin in the garage and stuck a Christmas tree in the chimney. We didn't notice until the following day, by which time everyone had seen it and was laughing at us. He hated New Year's Eve and muffled the doorbell with cardboard, taped up the letterbox and lifted the garden gate off its hinges and put it in the shed. Then, he would lay down tripwires of string everywhere and go on about fireworks. They were a public nuisance and shouldn't be allowed. How many thatched houses would be burnt down this year? And what about the fingers lost and eyes damaged?

The Hagenmüller family came to visit for the New Year once – with their sons, Axel, Rainer and Claus. It was a fantastic sight, watching Uncle Helmut's car drive up Hans Ditlevsensgade. It was much bigger than ours, but Father said that ours cost four times as much because of import taxes. If we had lived in Germany, we would have had a Mercedes 500! We fetched Grandmother from the station, and Axel took her suitcase, Rainer opened the door, and Claus sat himself beside her in the back and sucked up to her. They were only doing it for the sweets and money, to screw her for what they could get and to take my Grandmother away from me, and I found myself wishing that they would all go to hell. It didn't cross my mind that in a way this was where they had come.

Mother laid the table with the Meissner. We were to have lobster and champagne and Danish marzipan ring cake. She had bought streamers and paper hats – and, best of all, fireworks! They were fun, she said, and evil spirits should be driven out of the house over New Year. Father sighed, and I looked forward to midnight all evening. The atmosphere was unpleasant. Father compared Danish and German prices for everything under the sun and went on about taxes and duties. Helmut shook his head in amazement that they could be so high in Denmark. It really was incredible. The most important thing was to avoid any mention of sensitive issues, especially inheritance.

Papa Schneider had died without writing a will, and Eva was his direct descendant, related by blood – she was a '*blutsverwandt*' – and therefore, in principle, the sole heir. When compensation for losses in East Germany came through at last – '*Entschädigung*' – Eva took the lot. It was beyond belief. How could she do it? And to her own mother and sister? It was as though the boil had burst. The grievances and accusations poured out of her – Grandmother had never loved her father, had only married him for his money, she had never been a love-child as Mother had been – Hilde was '*Tochter des hochgeliebten Heinrich Voll*', while she was '*Tochter des nicht so hochgeliebten Papa Schneider*' – and Mother had stolen all her men from her and ruined her life! She shouted and screamed and became hysterical – and they got no more than the 8 per cent they were entitled to – not a penny more – and Mother gave her share to Grandmother and swore to take revenge.

At midnight we heard the chimes from the tower of City Hall in Copenhagen on the polished mahogany radio – it had been plugged in for the occasion – and raised our fine cut glasses and toasted each other, Eva and Helmut, Axel, Rainer and Claus and Grandmother. And Father said 'Steady!' and 'Careful now' as I clinked glasses with Mother. She smoked her cheroots and said that now it was party time, took out the bag with the fireworks and went out into the street – and then she let off the rockets. She lit the fuses with her glowing cheroot, and they whistled up to explode far above, filling the sky with a sea of stars and golden rain – and the tears rolled down Grandmother's cheeks.

'*Ach, wie schön!*'

People came outside to watch. There were Shooting Stars and Catherine Wheels and the Golden Rain cascaded up and threw out their sprays of flowers to crackle down upon us. It ended with a single massive detonation, and when all was still again, we could hear a whining sound that went on and on and came from inside the house. It was Eva – she had got a shock during a bombing raid and had never got over it. She was standing in the dining room, white as a sheet and petrified, her screams piercing the air like a crack fracturing the porcelain.

They slaughtered him, Mother said, Horst Heilmann – her Horstchen. He was executed and hanged from a meathook. Her voice hurt. It belonged to another woman. She lived inside Mother and had died long since. I was afraid of her and hid in my room when she came out, when her eyes turned cold and distant and looked at me from the other side of the grave.

Mother drank to keep her at bay and that only made it worse. Each time she emptied a vodka bottle, it would be an execution. '*Vollstreckt,*' she would say – and her eyes looked out at a grey December day in Berlin in 1942. Behind the walls and the iron doorway stood the Plötzensee prison, the buildings and yards made impregnable by barbed wire, railings and iron bars. The floors of death row were polished till they shone, and down the middle ran a strip of green linoleum that no one was ever allowed to walk on. It was smooth as glass – '*blitzblank*' – and it was awful.

In front of the cell doors stood the stools with prisoners' clothing ordered with rigorous military precision. Trousers, jacket, socks – bowl on top, shoes beneath. The lighting was subdued – they were economizing because of the war – and the place was silent and comfortless. Inside the cells sat Horst and Harro and Libertas and Arvid and Mildred and others from the *Rote Kapelle*, waiting to be fetched, each sending out silent pleas for help, knowing that it was hopeless.

Some of them had tried to get away, hoping to escape their fate. Rudolf von Scheliha arranged a meeting at Café Krantzler on the pretext of denouncing a Soviet agent. He ordered a cup of coffee and waited. Then he suddenly got up, concealed himself behind a guest who was on his way to the toilet, and ran – out through the kitchen door and straight into the arms of the police, who stood there laughing at him. Ilse Stöbe hatched one plan of escape after the other, trying everything, including having sex with one of the prison guards who was supposed to help her get out. He, too, was hanged.

Schulze-Boysen tried a ruse to play for time. He told them that he had posted documents to Stockholm that presented a serious threat to the German military. He would reveal what this was and tell the truth, if they guaranteed

– in his father's presence – to delay his execution. It was a desperate throw of the dice that depended on the imminent collapse of the German Front. The Russian counter-offensive was under way, and the USA had declared war. Superintendent Panzinger agreed to the proposal, and his father was summoned – he was an officer in the navy and was related to Admiral Alfred von Tirpitz. Harro played his card – explained that the truth about the documents in Stockholm was that there were none – and the deal was off.

A radio message from Moscow to the agent in Brussels – 'Kent' – had put German intelligence on their track. They picked it up in October 1941 but were not able to break the code until six months later when the Gestapo managed to arrest the operator, Johann Wenzel. He broke under torture and gave them the key to the secret messages. There were addresses and telephone numbers of three contacts in Berlin, among them Schulze-Boysen.

Horst Heilmann worked in the intelligence services and, when he found out that they had been discovered and were under surveillance, he tried to warn Harro and John Graudenz and the others, but it was too late. On Monday 31st August Schulze-Boysen was arrested at the Ministry of Aviation and five days later they arrested Horst on Matthäikirchplatz. Over the weeks that followed Himmler cracked down hard – they rounded up suspects in Berlin and right across Germany – and over 120 were sent to the cellars of the Gestapo jails on Prince Albrecht Straße and Moabit.

The prosecutor-general presented the case before the Reich's court martial in Berlin-Charlottenburg on 15th

December 1942: 'In the name of the People: The evidence supports the conclusion that this organization did not respect certain crucial secrets concerning Germany's military strategy. No one can fail to be struck with horror at the thought that Germany's secrets have been exposed to the eyes of the enemy.'

The courtroom was sparsely furnished, and Horst and Harro and Libertas sat between policemen with ten of the other main defendants. Their faces were hollow. There were only a few observers, most of them in uniform – the Nazis preferred to avoid a show trial because the number and the prominence of members of the resistance movement were both an embarrassment and a danger to them. It was declared a secret state matter – there was not even any notification in the press – and the charge was high treason.

As many of the accused were military personnel – Schulze-Boysen was an officer in the *Luftwaffe* – the case came before a court martial, and the judges were two generals and an admiral; a president of the senate was chairman and there was a civilian legal assessor. The prosecutor was Senior Judge Advocate Manfred Roeder, notorious for his contempt for mankind, his coldness, his brutality. He was the Nazis' henchman, ruthlessly punishing the least resistance to the regime as high treason, and they knew straight away that they were going to die.

Arvid Harnack made no secret of his convictions and for twenty minutes spoke in his own defence. He admitted that he regarded the Soviet Union as the world's only bulwark against Nazism and concluded by saying that his aim had been the annihilation of the Hitler state by any means available: *'Die Vernichtung des Hitlerstaates mit allen Mitteln war mein Ziel.'* His voice was quiet and tired, and he spoke almost as though it were a formality, as though he had already resigned himself, but some of the other accused fought to the last. Schulze-Boysen confessed to what could not be denied and denied whatever Roeder could not prove, reckoning that the Gestapo had not arrested the entire organization. Rushing the arrests had meant that a large number of individuals had slipped through the net, and time and again they were without crucial middlemen from the extended European network – 'Kent', Fritz Bock, Paul Robinson, Gilbert, the radio operators, the couriers, the Russian agents. If they were mentioned at all, it was not with their real names, and no torture could force the prisoners at Prinz-Albrecht-Straße to reveal them because they didn't know them.

The trial lasted for four days, and Erika von Brockdorff – blonde and elegant – laughed when Roeder demanded a sentence of death. That laugh, he snapped, will soon fade from your lips.

'Ihnen wird das Lachen schon vergehen.'

Not as long as she could see him, came the reply. She was removed from the courtroom. But she was right and was sentenced to six years, and Mildred also got off with a prison sentence. However, Hitler refused to ratify their sentences, and after a fresh trial both were condemned to death. As were they all. Forty-five people ended on the scaffold, the women beheaded by guillotine, the men hanged – and the only comment Horst Heilmann made to his sentence was a wish to die beside his friend: *'Ich möchte mit Schulze-Boysen gemeinsam sterben dürfen.'*

Two days before Christmas Eve – on 22nd December 1942 – the first eleven resistance people were executed in Plötzensee prison between 8.18 and 8.33 in the evening. Those sentenced to death were taken to the wing leading off from Ward III, which gave onto a small courtyard. At the end of this there was a low-ceilinged building with a whitewashed and windowless room, across the middle of which hung a black curtain. Behind the curtain stood the guillotine and against the back wall there were smaller cells with black curtains where the hangings took place.

During his last hours Arvid Harnack sat with his hands bound behind his back, listening to the prologue in heaven from Goethe's *Faust*, which the priest read aloud for him, and his American wife, Mildred, translated poems by Rilke into English in her death cell. Hilde Coppi breast-fed her son. Harro Schulze-Boysen wrote a farewell letter to his parents:

Have faith as I do in the time that will come, when justice will be done. For the fact is that in Europe, spiritually, seeds of blood are being sown. Yes, and now I reach out my hand to you all and place here one tear (and only one) as a seal and pledge of my love.

Your Harro

One by one they were taken from the death wing and led across the courtyard and into the cold hall of execution.

Against the long wall of the hall stood an old table, and behind this stood the public prosecutor. There were ten, maybe fifteen witnesses – some of them embarrassed, appalled, others curious, arrogant or vindictive – and none of them said a word. Opposite them were the hangmen, the chief executioner in a silk top hat, the others in black suits. In 1942 executions were no longer accompanied by a ceremony – there had been too many of them. The most important thing was to get it over as quickly as possible.

'Are you Harro Schulze-Boysen?' asked the public prosecutor as the first prisoner entered, his arms tied behind his back. *Jawohl,'* he said – dry, defiant, hard.

'I deliver you over for the execution of the death sentence.'

They took off the jacket that hung over his naked shoulders, and he made a sign to the guards holding him that he would rather walk alone. They released him, and, walking upright in his worn-out slippers, he crossed to the ramp, where a leather strop hung from a meat-hook.

To ensure a painful and humiliating death, Hitler had ordered that they should be hung from a meat-hook, and the gallows with eight hooks was built specially for them. Harro Schulze-Boysen stepped up onto the ramp and looked down at the witnesses, his eyes full of contempt – and then the black curtain was drawn. The man with the silk hat stepped out of the cell – for a moment they could see the jerking of the body – and the curtain fell again behind the hangman. He stepped forward before the public prosecutor and declared: *'Das Urteil ist vollstreckt.'* The sentence has been executed. And raised his arm in a Hitler salute.

As though on cue, the door of the hall opened, and the next condemned entered between two guards. *'Sie sind Arvid Harnack?'* – *'Jawohl'* – *'Das Urteil ist vollstreckt'* – *'Sie sind John Graudenz?'* – *'Jawohl'* – *'Das Urteil ist vollstreckt'* – *'Sie sind Kurt Schumacher?'* – *'Jawohl'* – *'Das Urteil ist vollstreckt'* – *'Sie sind Hans Coppi?'* – *'Jawohl'* – *'Das Urteil ist vollstreckt'* – *'Sie sind Kurt Schultze?'* – *'Jawohl'* – *'Das Urteil ist vollstreckt'* – *'Sie sind Herbert Gollnow?'* – *'Jawohl'* – *'Das Urteil ist vollstreckt'* – *'Sie sind Elisabeth Schumacher?'* – *'Jawohl'* – *'Das Urteil ist vollstreckt'* – *'Sie sind Libertas Schulze-Boysen?'* – *'Jawohl'* *'Das Urteil ist vollstreckt'* – and so they were murdered and no one said a word.

They were hung like pigs in a slaughterhouse, Mother said, and she emptied the vodka bottle and thought about Horstchen. *'Das Urteil ist vollstreckt.'* The pain in her voice was shrill and sharp and it cut its way out of her face and pierced me to the heart as she stared at me, and I was ready to die with terror. Not knowing who she was.

The town's school stood beside the Guldborg casting foundry, and the ash from the chimney drifted across the playground, covering the buildings in smuts and spreading like confetti. It got into everything – in your hair, your clothes, your books, and made your hands filthy – and when it rained, the soot dribbled down your face and the puddles were black.

It was not a school I went to. It was a penitentiary, and every day I had to learn my lesson. The teachers would come in and take their place behind the lectern. We sat at our desks – I had one for myself – and then we had dictation and the red lines criss-crossed our exercise books. It didn't matter which subject we had – History, Danish, Geography, Maths – they were all about the same thing, and that was keeping up and doing as you were told, and if you wouldn't learn the easy way you could learn the hard way and get a clip across the ear and be sent down to the remedial class where the children had lice.

By and large school was about sitting still and parroting every word – the Volga, the Danube, and Gudenå, and two-plus-two-is-four – and most important of all were patriotism and hating the Germans. In History we had sermons about 1864 and the Battle of Dybbøl Mølle – all seen in the light of the war – and we heard about the Danish resistance, the Churchill Club, about Montgomery and the concentration camps. The teacher shook his head. Inhuman it was. When the map was rolled down in front of the blackboard in Geography, each country had a colour – Germany was black, the Soviet Union was red and it was Denmark all the way down to the Eider. In Danish lessons we read Danish resistance songs like *Stjernerne vil lyse*, and the Germans were always the baddies in the *Jan* detective club as they were in all the books in the school library. In Music Frøken Møller sat at the piano, warming us up with patriotic hymns – *Venner, ser på Danmarks Kort* and *Danmark mellem tvende Have* – before warbling *Det haver så nyligen regnet*.[5] Everyone joined in, for she had been in the resistance and had smuggled a hand grenade in her handbag across Christian IX's Bridge during the occupation!

When the bell went, it marked the start of break for the others and the end of break for me, and I would try to survive until class started again. They had learned their lessons and they knew what I was. I was the German pig, and Mother was a Hitler bitch and Mrs Manager and stuck-up and lah-di-dah, until the wet seeped down my thighs. I spent most of my time standing at the centre of a circle – boys and girls – as they shoved and spat and shouted in time. The worst of it was when they made fun of Mother and brayed 'Hilde-gaaaard, Hilde-gaaaard' just like goats and fell about laughing hysterically. It grated in my ears and I was ashamed and refused to answer when anyone asked me what her name was. Then it was under the water-pump before the bell went again – the teacher stood with his back to the wall and did nothing and had seen nothing – and I was late for class and soaked and was told off. Had I peed my pants, perhaps? The class collapsed in laughter, and I was sent home to change.

There was someone else in Class B who also copped it – Nina Westphal. She had long, dark hair and her father was an invalid, he had multiple sclerosis, and sat in a wheelchair. They teased her about it and, even though she was a girl, they went for her, did her over – her father was a spazzer!

[5] These are four famous nationalistic Danish songs. Their titles can be rendered: '*The stars will shine*', '*Friends, the map of Denmark see*', '*Denmark between the oceans twain*' and '*The rain and the storm have abated*' – *trans.*

I watched her sitting on her own in the window sill, falling more and more to pieces with every year that passed. She had nervous tics, her eyes glazed over, she started behaving strangely and would overreact at the slightest provocation – and then she was gone. I don't know whether they moved away from Nykøbing or whether she was sent somewhere else, but Nina had got away – and there was nothing I wanted more than to do the same.

I read the Jennings novels and dreamt that it was me that had been sent to boarding school, but every time I came home and refused to go back, I was met with a 'No'. Just wait and see, things would soon improve, and I was to stick it out for now and I would get whatever I wanted. What I wanted was pancakes, Coca-Cola, Donald Duck comics. When I got them, back I went again – fifth, sixth, seventh year – until one day I pushed my bike out of the playground and Mother was standing in the gateway in her ocelot. I was taken aback and asked what she was doing there. She said I should just go on home, and then she caught sight of Michael – he was one of the worst – and chased him down the road in her fur coat and high-heeled shoes. I couldn't bear to watch and biked off, knowing full well what was in store for me the next day at school – and they would be waiting with electrician's rods and hooks, Jørgen and Poul and Jesper with Michael at the head – and I might just as well stand up against the wall and wait to be shot.

The only thing I associated Nykøbing with was fear. I did not dare go out on the streets and usually had to make a wide detour if I wanted to go anywhere – and always arrived late. I couldn't use Grønsundsvej because that took me past the Jæger Grill, where they would be standing revving their mopeds – Puch 3-speed for the boys with Easy Rider handlebars and high seatbacks, Puch Maxis for the girls – and they wore blue denim jackets with a hairbrush stuffed in the front pocket. The girls were always brushing their hair with them, while the boys used them to hit you with – your blood welled up in the perforated patterns. I had been through it too often. I had gone in there with Father to buy half a grilled chicken with chips – that was what we did when Mother wasn't home – and Stinky John and Jesper and Sten stood by the jukebox gawping at us. They began talking in loud voices about '*Sauer Krauts*' and how Germans were '*Würst*', making sound like 'worst' – and Sten came over to us and gave me a shove. And when Father said, 'Steady on. What do you think you're doing?' he just laughed. We took our insulated bag with the chicken and the tray of chips and drove home. I couldn't eat anything but watched Father and hoped he would kill them.

'Crazy Johanne's coming! Crazy Johanne's coming!'

The children shouted and screamed, word running several streets ahead of her when she came staggering through the town dragging behind her a tail of stench. She was dressed in rags and worn-out shoes and you could hardly see her for all the cloths wrapped round her head – if, that was, you dared look in her direction. She had a sack slung over her shoulder and stared fixedly ahead saying, 'Go 'way, go 'way, go 'way!' We were horror-struck, shrieked and fled in all directions as soon as she appeared round the corner. Her house was on Østre Allé – the windows were boarded over, and weeds and piles of rubbish spread in wild profusion behind the fence. If you threw stones and shouted 'Crazy Johanne! Crazy Johanne!' she would come charging out with an axe above her head and scream at you, and I kept well away.

Nor could I take Bispegade and sneak past the large red buildings of the Technical School, where I risked being attacked, especially in winter when it had snowed. The snowballs were hard. They stung and ripped the blood out of your cheeks because they were packed with grit. The streets around Østre School were dangerous, and it wasn't safe to use the tunnel. That would otherwise be the quickest route going directly under the railway tracks, but they would be lying in wait down there – it was impossible to get away. And every time I had to go into town I avoided the station and went the long way round under the bridge and up Vesterskovvej.

On Frisegade there was the inn. Paul Fisker would hit anything that moved when he was drunk and on Saturdays they had a stripper – and I hurried down Slotsgade with my heart in my mouth because there was the risk that I might run into Tommy. He lived at the back of a shop with his father and cleaned typewriters. He was a young offender and drove at 75 kilometres an hour on his moped, which was tuned and bored and stroked and re-geared. Tommy was the leader of the pack from the moment he walked into the classroom – that was in seventh year – and the girls were wild about him, drawing hearts and writing 'Tommy' in flower-power letters on their pencil cases. He hung out with the rockers along with Gert, who stammered and had psoriasis – and rumour had it that he had gone looking for his mother on her birthday, had dragged her out of the shower and beaten her up. They had insignia on their jackets and became members of the Wizards, who had their base in a cellar on Strandgade, and that made the whole of the southern part of the harbour a no-go zone. So was Lindeskoven, where they were building new high-rise flats out of concrete – that was where the youth club was. The boys wore Slade hair. They smoked and drank beer and listened to Gasolin, while the girls wore flares and clogs and listened to the Walker Brothers – and I never crossed Gedservej.

When the fair came to Nykøbing it set up on a square they called The Cement. It flashed and was noisy as a toyshop – dodgems and swingboats, shooting galleries, one-armed bandits – and there was ice cream in cones and popcorn that smelt of sausages. But it was out of bounds. The one time I had dared to go in to hear Sir Henry on the open-air stage, some of the Wizards were there. Gert recognized me and got the others to hold me as he pissed on my trousers. Even by day I was afraid to go anywhere near the discotheques where they had their parties – The Scarlet Pimpernel, Ellen's Ranch – and on Fridays they would gather at the station and warm up by the pool in the park at Svanedammen. I never went into town after dark.

The boys played in the B 1901 football team, and on Saturdays there were matches at the stadium. I didn't dare go, and Father said that football was only for idiots. I bought liquorice balls and allsorts in the kiosk and watched the girls play handball down in the Sports Hall. They wore NFH for Nykøbing Falster Handball, and I was in love with Susanne who was blonde. I hid from Stinky John, who went to wrestling. His wrestling kit was never washed and he stank like a shit-heap – his smell hit me before he did – and I almost threw up when he punched me in my guts and never went to the Sports Hall again.

The last past the post was thrown on the scrap, and when we chose teams I was always left till last. I was shoved into the water when we went swimming, and my shoes and socks were stolen from the changing rooms. I shook my head, refusing to go with the others into Skårup's garden to steal apples – there was a shed that was used as a meeting point, where they dished out punishments – and in the summer I didn't go with the others to the beach. The last time I had gone, they had prepared a trap. Susanne was coming, too, they told me – she wanted to ask me something. And we cycled out with trunks and towels on our bike racks. The road took us through Lindeskov wood, and fields and meadows spread out on either side under a blue sky as we turned to the left along the main road that wound through Tjæreby and Stovby and on to Marielyst. The sun baked down. The air shimmered over the sea-wall. We changed in a hollow and raced each other down to the water – only I fell in a hole filled to the brim with stinging jellyfish.

They had spread sand over it to make it invisible, and they kept pushing me back, stopping me from crawling out, until they got tired of it and let me get away when they went for a swim. I fetched my things and cycled off, my skin on fire with the burns, and made a wide circuit around Kjørup's inn and Marielyst Market, where they had holiday jobs – the ice cream kiosk, the camping site, the minigolf. They overcharged and made fun of the tourists and crowed with delight every time a German was carried out to sea on a lilo and drowned – and I continued all the way out to Elkenøre, which would be empty of people.

For the school party the gym would be decorated and a bar with lemonade and Coke was set up in one of the class-rooms with a cloakroom in another. In the junior classes we had marched in in procession, hand in hand, and danced 'Oh, Boogie Woogie Woogie' in a long chain, but now we could decide for ourselves. The boys came along with beer in plastic bags – Blå Nykøbing lager – and the girls hid a bottle of red Martini in the toilets and were constantly going in and out to put on blue eye shadow and brush their hair. I had been in love with Susanne since the first year. Her father was a baker a few streets away on Solvej – the sign of the pretzel hung over the door and once in a while she would stand behind the counter. I used to call on her every Sunday, would ring the doorbell and asked if Susanne was home. You had to be quiet because her father would be asleep – he got up early – and we would watch television in the living room with her mother with the sound turned right down. I would wait for her to say it – 'Shall we go to my room?' – and would sit beside Susanne on the divan bed for hours not knowing how to go about it, how I was to give her a kiss. Maybe it would be best to ask? Or maybe if I put my arm around her and held her hand? Nothing ever came of it – not even when we said goodbye, for she closed the door before I managed to kiss her – and then I'd be standing there the following Sunday, ringing the bell, and the one after that, and at long last I decided to go along to the party.

The gym was in semi-darkness. There were Danish flags and paper chains, the disco lights were flashing, and there was the smell of sweat and rancid towels and plimsolls. The boys were propped against the wall bars on one side of the hall, the girls sat on benches on the other side, and the music played to an empty floor – Bay City Rollers for the girls, Nazareth and Status Quo for the boys – and everyone was waiting for things to get going. And they did with 'Hey, We're Going to Barbados!' The flight captain was greeting the passengers – 'Captain Tobias Wilcox welcoming passengers aboard Coconut Airways Flight 372 to Bridgetown!' – and the girls got up and began to dance cautiously with each other in a huddle. Before the song was over, the first boys were dancing, too, and the rest joined them to 'New York Groove' with Hello, and then it was 'Sugar Baby Love' with The Rubettes and 'Magic' with Pilot, and then came Mud and Showaddywaddy, and the dance drew towards its close and the time for the highpoint of the evening – the slow shuffle.

I had promised myself that I would do it and looked round for Susanne. They were playing 'If You Think You Know How To Love Me' with Smokey, and that was the sign. And then over by the door to the gym I saw that Tommy and Michael had pitched up with some of the others from the youth club. The rest of them remained standing by the door as Tommy strolled over to the girls. Then he took Susanne out onto the floor for the slow shuffle. During the next number – 'I'm Not in Love' by 10cc – they started snogging, and so it went on and on, but I couldn't get away because I had to get past the others standing in the doorway, and Michael had caught sight of me. There was no way out of it, and none of it mattered anyway – Susanne had her hand inside Tommy's trousers. And now it was Gilbert O'Sullivan with 'Alone Again, Naturally' – and I just wanted to die and get it over with once and for all, and I grabbed a bottle and rushed headlong for the exit.

For as long as I can remember I have been looking for a way out of Nykøbing and out of the house where I grew up. I couldn't go anywhere, and I was always on my guard, trying to squeeze into the tightest space – it was like walking a tightrope – and the street was the width of my footstep and went from our garage to school and back again. It all gathered and hardened into a stone in my pocket – it was an eaglestone and rattled and Father said that it came from the chalk sea, but no one knew how one stone came to be inside another one – and I added it to the collection in my drawer.

Here I kept conch shells and fossilized sea urchins and old ham sandwiches wrapped in foil and the fragments of grenade Uncle Helmut had given me alongside all the other stuff I squirrelled away and kept to myself. I collected everything. It had to be there somewhere. I'd find it all right – happiness waiting just round the corner. It was just like at Easter. All you had to do was follow your nose – you were warmer or colder and now burning hot – and there it was, one egg in the bookcase, one under the lamp and another in the centrepiece on the dining table. When we went for a woodland walk with Grandmother in Hamborgskoven you'd see things glinting in the long grass and find eggs left by the Easter bunny wrapped in yellow and red and blue silver paper.

'*Der Osterhase war da,*' she would say, pointing to the trail – and I would almost believe it.

It was one long drawn-out treasure-hunt, and I followed the clues – they were everywhere – looking for four-leafed clover in the garden, for coins in the street that usually turned out to be flattened blobs of chewing gum, but you never knew, sifting through piles of gravel looking for fulgurites – they came from lightning strikes, and you got a shock when you found one – and in the evenings I looked for shooting stars. I cycled out to Falkerslev in gumboots and looked for flint axes and arrowheads when the fields had been ploughed, and I went down to the harbour and lay on the quay wall looking down into the water. It smelt of

tar and rotting seaweed, and I counted the minnows swimming round in shoals and fished for crabs with a flounder's
head tied to a string.

There were hazelnuts in our neighbours' garden – Herr
and Fru Hansen. He worked at the foundry and coughed
all the time. And I collected chestnuts from the bishop's
garden, the shells of edible snails, rings used for marking
hens, marbles. Uncle Helmut gave me lumps of quartz and
a fossil – a petrified octopus called an ammonite – and they
all joined the other pieces in my exhibition on the shelf.

For me there was nothing better than stamps. They
swarmed in cardboard boxes like butterflies – and the afternoons rolled into one when I sat sorting them in the dining-
room. They were windows into a world that was larger and
richer than anyone could imagine. It was full of crowned
heads and foreign countries like Helvetia, Suomi and – most
beautiful of all – Formosa, which was out there somewhere,
waiting with its parrots and orchids and pink clouds. I tried
to find it, travelling round the world, seeing the pyramids
and travelling on trains – and then *par avion* to Thule and
onward by frigate to Italy. I was at the Olympics in Mexico,
greeted King Frederik IX dressed in red and only realized
how late it was when the special Christmas stamps twinkled
at the bottom and I came back to earth, put the lid on the
box and was already looking forward to tomorrow.

I was sure that I was on the track of a tremendous secret,
went creeping round the house exploring as they did in
The Famous Five and *Emil and the Detectives*. I investigated,
tapping on walls in the hallway and listening to discover the

secret door that had to be there and sounded hollow. The most frightening place was the boiler room – the sounds of the boiler came up through the floor of my bedroom – and I peopled it with hanged men and black cats playing cards and all the worst scenes from Grimm's fairy tales. Many years were to pass before I dared go down there. I opened the door and fumbled for the light switch – you never knew what might jump at you out of the dark – but it was just a warm, grey room with the boiler chuntering away in the corner. There was nothing to be afraid of – a lathe, garden chairs, cardboard boxes full of shoes, newspapers and odds and ends that Father had tidied up and put away – you never knew when things might come in handy – and behind the curtain an ancient trunk.

It was the sort that people used to travel to America with – black and battered and big enough to sit inside – and on the lid a pair of initials written in gothic script: 𝔍.𝔖. It was Papa Schneider's trunk. I was dying to know what was inside and knocked – there was a moment when I was afraid he would open it and stick his head out – but it was locked. It must have been filled with treasure. Perhaps Papa Schneider had been a big game hunter? I saw him before me in white topee out on the savannah. Or else he'd be standing on deck in evening dress on board an ocean liner. The trunk had ended up in our cellar for one reason and one reason only – to fetch me and ferry me across the Atlantic.

I only had to find the key, and I knew where to look but did not dare pursue the thought to its conclusion. The bureau. It stood in the living room and was for cut glass, important documents and valuables. A bronze clock had been placed on top of it and there were porcelain figures on the writing flap that could fall off. I wasn't allowed to open the drawers or the door – I was sure it had a secret compartment. In it was the answer to all mysteries. I was frightened of being caught in the act and put it off so long that in the end I could not stop myself, and it happened all by itself.

As soon as Mother had gone to grocer Olsen's to do the shopping, I got going. I was like a burglar – everything felt different, alien – and I had to move fast. What I had to do was move the figures in order to get at the drawers and then put them back precisely as they had stood before so that no one could see they had been moved. I listened. Was there anyone at the door? Footsteps on the cellar stairs? The bronze clock ticked louder and louder. I leafed through old passports, certificates of baptism, family trees and papers stamped in blue, black, red, some of them with the German eagle. There was a jewellery box. There were the gold coins I had been given by Dr Jaschinski for my birthday, photos of Farmor and Grandfather in front of the bus and of the family in Kleinwanzleben. I didn't look like Grandfather and turned to Karen. So there she was. She looked serious. And not daring to breathe for fear of discovery, I opened the little door in the bureau.

A brown envelope lay there, with the words '*Erinnerungen von Hildchen*' written in Mother's hand. I opened it carefully. It was full of photographs of her mother and her father, Heinrich Voll, school reports, sports diploma – tennis, swimming, riding – her pass from the *Arbeitsdi-*

enst – '*Arbeit für dein Volk adelt dich selbst*' – and a questionnaire for the denazification of Hannover. I didn't have time to look at them properly but continued my search and found a folded letter. It was from Horst Heilmann. It was dated Berlin 20.8.42, and at the top in block capitals he had written '*Geheim/Vernichten*'. *Secret/Destroy*. The rest was in a sloping hand, and I couldn't read it, but it was not for my eyes anyway. Then there was a wish list for Mother's first Christmas at Papa Schneider's:

Liebes Christkind! Ich bin das Hildchen Voll und wohne in Kleinwanzleben. Ich wünsche mir ein Puppenwagen und Nüsse, Äpfel und Pfefferkuchen aber auch ein Weihnachtsbaum wo wir zu Weihnachten herum stehen und singen o, du fröhliche es wird ganz herrlich werden. Aber ich weiss ja gar nicht wo ich meine Schularbeiten machen soll dann wünsche ich mir noch ein Schreibpult. Aber zum kneten auch noch ein Kasten Knetgummi. Mein Vorleger vors Bettchen ist ganz zerissen könnte ich nicht einen neuen haben? Und zum Kochen einen kleinen Weckapparat. Zum Lesen ein Buch. Und einen neuen Roller. [6]

It had a red stamp on which a cherub was singing and printed on it the words *Gloria in excelsis deo, 5 Pfennig*. It

---

[6] Dear Christ child! I am little Hilde Voll and I live in Kleinwanzleben. I would like a doll's pram and nuts and apples and peppercakes but also a Christmas tree that we can stand around in a ring and sing *o du fröhliche* it will be so lovely. But I have no idea where I am going to do my homework so I would also like a desk. But I would also like some Plasticene to make figures with. My bedside rug is all worn could I have a new one? And a little stove. And a book to read. And a new scooter with a rubber wheel. And some sweeties, too.

was strange to think that Mother had been so small. I was thinking about Hildchen Voll as I picked up the box that lay right at the back, lifted the lid and was struck by a thunderbolt. There it was, the crock of gold at the end of the rainbow, the buried treasure – and it was death. The Iron Cross. The black cast-iron cross was inlaid with silver with crossed swords and a swastika in the centre. It was Mother's – and then I heard the key turn in the front door.

For years I thought they were right, that Mother was a Nazi, and I was ashamed and defended her. But it wasn't true. Mother had been decorated by General Raegener – this was after the war – and she was given it for rescuing hundreds of German soldiers from Russian deportation. It was Uncle Helmut who told me. When I finally plucked up the courage to ask Mother, she said that she had wound the head of the sector for the Red Cross round her little finger – a Mr Plaiter – and he got himself drunk on gin, declared his undying love and promoted her to 'Chief clerk' for the ambulance service, as she had asked him to. Then she organized the escape, using the ambulances to smuggle soldiers from the hospital over the Elbe and into the West. She had not been able to save Horstchen but she had managed to ferry as many others to safety as possible – and it was deadly dangerous, for they could have rumbled her at any moment. When the military police came for her, Mother nodded and fetched her coat. But they were only asking her to report to the American high command. She was not arrested. They didn't say what it was all about, and Mother took a gamble and went. It was General Raegener who had sent for her. He was a prisoner of war, and there was something he wished to talk to her about. He walked into the visiting room with his wooden leg, shook hands and said thank you – and then he took out a box and handed her the Iron Cross Second Class.

It was hidden away in a box with the black-white-and red ribbon of the order. She never took it out or discussed it with anyone. I had only seen her wear it once and that was in 1967. It was the World Fair in Montreal. Mother and Father were on their grand tour to Canada and saw Niagara Falls and visited the Lions Club in Chicago on the way back. Shortly after this they were excluded from the local branch in Nykøbing – it was not 'international' enough to be able to accept a Nazi, as they put it – and Mother hit the roof when they returned in the evening from the Baltic Hotel. She went across to the bureau, took out the box and pinned on the Iron Cross. Then she left the house, Father standing in the hall in the light falling from the living room – and I tried to prevent her, to get her to leave it be and to stop. But it wasn't her anymore. She couldn't hear a word anyone said but walked up Grønsundsvej to Højbroen, over the bridge and all the way through the town wearing the Iron Cross and singing 'Das Preußenlied' all the way:

Ich bin ein Preuße, kennt ihr meine Farben?
Die Fahne schwebt mir weiß und Schwarz voran!

Daß für die Freiheit meine Väter starben,
Das deuten, merkt es, meine Farben an.
Nie werd' ich bang verzagen,
Wie jene will ich's wagen:
Sei's trüber Tag, sei's heitrer Sonnenschein,
Ich bin ein Preuße, will ein Preuße sein! [7]

Father was at a loss as to what to say or how to explain it.
At dinner not a word was said about it, and Mother served us
Maccaroniauflauf. She could fall to pieces at any moment. I
walked on eggshells, supported her as best I could, nodding
and playing along. That was quite right, and yes, of course.
Whenever I wanted to go out, Mother would ask *'Wo gehst
du hin?'* and I would have to say where and promise to be
back before long and, if I was late, she would be beside
herself – where had I been? I hurried home and shouted
'Hi!' on my way up the stairs from the cellar, hoping she
was in a good mood. Her voice was full of reproaches, she
was worried, and even the most ordinary things became
artificial, felt awkward, sounded like lines rehearsed. She
transformed everything around her into a tragedy, and we
took up our roles and appeared in her performance, while
the dining room, the table, the paintings were all just props.
If one of us had spoken out of character and told the truth,
hell would have been let loose. We were possessed by an evil

[7] 'A Prussian, I. Can you see my colours fly?/Ahead the flag is waving black and
white./For freedom did our fathers fight and die,/ That is the message that my
colours write./ Never will my heart despair;/One and all we Prussians dare./ In
brightest sunlight and in darkest rain/ A Prussian I, and Prussian will remain!'

spirit, and Father sat at the dining table and asked for the salt and in desperation tried to think of an insurance scheme that would make it go away by itself.

But it wouldn't. Mother dreamed of settling accounts and had once seen the camp leader from *Arbeitsdienst* walking along by a railway station. She pretended she hadn't noticed her. What was she to do? Hit her? Spit at her? There was no such thing as justice. Mother did not believe in God. She hated him and drank extra strong lager and smoked cheroots and quoted Trakl. In silence above the site of the skull open God's golden eyes.

'Schweigsam über der Schädelstätte öffnen sich Gottes goldene Augen.'

And she would blow smoke at the ceiling and tell me how he had been acquitted after the war – Manfred Roeder, the state prosecutor who had murdered them all! He had personally ensured that those 'milksop' prison sentences for the women had been transmuted to the death sentence – for not having reported what was going on to the police. Even for Liane, and she was only nineteen. After the execution he rang Horst Heilmann's father to inform him – with contempt – that his son had been annihilated.

'Ihr Sohn ist ausgelöscht.'

And they sent a bill: 300 Reichsmark. Roeder had been doing his duty, the state prosecutor maintained and dismissed the case in 1951. The hangman was able to retire to his villa in Hessen and continue working as a solicitor, even becoming the chairman of the local parish council.

Rote Kapelle had never existed, said Mother, and she

could have taken the next train to Glashütten and slit his throat. It was the Gestapo who had invented the Communist spy ring in order to rid themselves of opponents of the regime. Roeder extended the web that was spun around the story and got the tribunal to believe that they had been agents and traitors to their country and deserved the death penalty. They had nothing whatsoever to do with the Soviet intelligence service. The radio transmitter didn't even work.

'*Ach!*' Mother sighed and stubbed out her cheroot.

And Schulze-Boysen had only sent one solitary message to Moscow, a blanket greeting to all friends. '*Tausend Grüße allen Freunden*'.

O nce the season got under way, the smoke billowed out of the chimney of the sugar factory The air smelt sweet and the snow fell to earth in sugared drops that tasted of boiled red sweets called 'Kings of Denmark'. I went around with my tongue stuck out, loving the snow and hating it. Fear rose inside me as softly as the snow that floated down and transformed the town into a great white battleground, where there was a good chance I would be attacked and clobbered. My head, my ears, my trousers would be filled with snow, I would eat snow in the breaks – and on the way home from school they would be lying in wait.

Tractors drove through the town with mountains of sugar beets. The children ran after them, waiting for some to fall off so that they could play with them – or sell them for a couple of crowns if there were enough. They would grow like mountains in front of the factory, and people would walk with their nose in the air, saying, 'It smells of money.' When they had parties, they became drunk on Blue Nykøbing lager and sang 'I come from Falster, where the wurzels grow, and they grow, and they grow and they grow! They grow and they grow – and they grow and they grow – and they grow and they grow and they grow!' It was nothing but wurzels from dawn till dusk.

One day Mother and I were shopping at grocer Olsen's. He was standing behind the counter and suddenly clutched his head and said, 'Oh, me wurzel hurts.' It suddenly struck me that they had wurzels instead of heads, too, and maybe this was just something that no one had told me.

I had a good look when I was at the baker's on Solvej, but Susanne smiled the same as always, and when we were out buying cheroots at the kiosk, I couldn't see anything unusual about the thin lady in front of me. And so I spent the rest of the day studying heads and looking for clues that might give them away – roots, traces of stalk. A lot of them did resemble wurzels when you took a closer look, and I grew more and more sure that I was right and felt queasy when the tractors drove past me on the street. I imagined that they were heads loaded on the trailers, and out on the fields they stood in earth up to their necks and they grew and they grew and they grew until they were harvested.

I had made an igloo on our drive and crawled inside, hiding, being a polar explorer in Greenland – Peter Freuchen had a street named after him just round the corner. It grew later than usual and I had dozed off in the darkness, when I heard someone laughing outside and crawled out to see who it was. A little further up the street stood a creature with a glowing head. Fire burned in its eyes, its nose, its mouth, and on the opposite side of the street I could see another flaming head. They were laughing at me with their triangular eyes and their evil smiles, and I screamed and ran and could hardly believe it – they had wurzels instead of heads and a light burning inside that you just couldn't see by day!

The secret of the sugar beet fields mushroomed. I had discovered something terrifying and I avoided them, averting my gaze and never looking them in the eye. The thickest boy in the class was called Jesper. He came from a farm outside town and wore shorts all year round. He had ringworm and a pudding-bowl haircut and ate pencils and picked his nose in class – and the more I studied him the more I was convinced that he was one of them.

Of course it wasn't long before I ran into him after school. He was sitting on a front step on Enighedsvej carving with his penknife and there were a number of smaller children watching. He looked up and said something or other to me, but I wasn't listening. I couldn't tear my eyes away from what he had in his hands. A wurzel! He had already cut the mouth and eyes.

'What you starin' at?' he asked and stood up.

I seized the opportunity.

'You're thick in the wurzel,' I replied and ran off as fast

as I could. He caught me up at once and knocked me down. The children flocked from all sides shouting 'Bat-tle! Bat-tle! Bat-tle!' while Jesper sat on top of me and gave me a clobbering, pushing my face in the snow until I couldn't breathe and was shouting for help!

Jesper stopped, looked down at me and said what they always said. 'German pig!' Then he laughed and the others all laughed along with him. I asked whether I could go now and was told that I had to beg first and say 'Please'. I nodded and raised myself carefully on my elbows, and before he knew what I was doing I had blown in his mouth. His eyes flickered, his arms flailed, and his face went out. Smoke came out of his ears, and then his head fell off and rolled down the street. The children ran away screaming. I knocked the snow off my coat, picked up the wurzel and went home to build a snowman. I put the wurzel on the top and the sight filled me with delight. Then I made a snowball and kept packing it tight until it was as hard as stone.

It was my fifteenth birthday, and Father told me to come with him out onto the street, and there it stood. A black 3-speed Puch. It didn't have high handlebars or backrest and had a top speed of only 30 kilometres an hour, and I had to wear a helmet that was yellow and twice the size of my head. I knew I would look ridiculous. 'Thanks a lot,' I said, and Mother asked whether I wasn't going to try it out. I trod on the kick-start and did a wheelie when I let in the clutch. Then I drove down Hans Ditlevsensgade and up Peter Freuchensvej and back again, and we went inside and had breakfast.

During the afternoon the doorbell rang – I started, fearing the worst – and outside stood Uncle Helmut. He had come all the way from Oberfranken. He was smaller and more bent than ever and he said *'Guten Tag!'* and wished me a happy birthday. We went up and joined Mother and Father in the dining-room, and I could see that it was difficult for him to walk.

'What a surprise!' said Father, and Mother poured him a cup of coffee and a cognac.

He said no to cake. He mustn't be late for the ferry. He went straight to the point and asked whether we could be alone for five minutes, and then he placed a piece of metal on the table. It was the last fragment of the hand grenade that had almost killed him. Uncle Helmut told me about Stalingrad, where they had been encircled by Russian forces and were staring defeat in the face. He was determined to desert because he was done no matter what happened, but he and his company managed to get through, and behind them the German army turned to ice.

I waved goodbye to Uncle Helmut, who hooted and turned the corner – and I never saw him again. As soon as he got home to Münchberg, he went into his clinic and took an X-ray of himself. It was what he was most frightened of. From it he could see that he was dying. He had got cancer – it was the X-rays – but he told no one and ate dinner as usual with Eva and Claus. Axel and Rainer had left home. After the meal he said *'Mahlzeit'* as always and dragged himself up the stairs to his room, where he closed the door and sat down with a bottle of wine and a glass of morphine. He began drinking as he wrote in his diary – he was convinced that his forefathers were standing there waiting for him in the next world – and when he had emptied his glass, Uncle Helmut fell asleep.

In the evening I climbed onto my scooter and drove out to the coast to see whether the sea was still there. It was. And there was nothing better than to end it all, standing on the edge of the Baltic, where the island of Falster ended, and to feel the wind buffeting your face. I looked out at the white-tipped waves breaking on the bar and walked along the beach – it stretched as far as the eye could see – looking for shells and fossilized sea-urchins and always hoping to find amber. It was so rare that it practically didn't exist. It was always just a piece of glass or a yellow pod of bladder-wrack. Nothing. I kicked up the sand and walked out on the breakwater, stretching my arms to either side and waving them up and down. It made the gulls fly off straight away. They thought I was a bird of prey. And I cursed the place and spat into the wind and felt my own spit slap back on my cheek.

E ven though I moved away from Nykøbing, I never left it, never escaped from the house on Hans Ditlevsens-gade. My parents lived alone with each other and sat listening to the grandfather clock marking time. It was the only thing that did. All else had ground to a halt. They had no one apart from me, and I was still '*das kleine Knüdchen*'. Every Christmas, New Year, Easter and birthday we celebrated together round the dining table, and everything was as it always had been.

The final years Father spent looking after Mother. An operation at a private hospital had gone wrong. They broke her back, and she couldn't straighten up. She walked at first with a stick, then with a Zimmer frame, fighting on and looking to me – her eyes tired and sad – but there was nothing I could do. She was inconsolable.

Mother grew more and more ill, complaining about chronic pains in her back and her bladder. She had a bladder infection that wouldn't go away, and she had to pee all the time and was given a catheter. Her throat was scorched by radiotherapy – she had got cancer of the mouth – and she ate less and less and was wasting away. The doctors could do nothing, couldn't even ease the pain – there was no morphine that worked – and then Mother fell and broke her leg. It was put in traction in a metal splint and she took to her bed, unable to move. They had their meals sent round and Father no longer went out of doors, living in the end in a house of no fixed abode. He didn't know where it was anymore. At times it was in Copenhagen, then it was in Orehoved or on Nybrogade in Nykøbing – and the world shrank into that one stuffy, dark and suffocating room furnished with the beds and the wardrobes from Kleinwanzleben.

One day Mother rang from the telephone in the bedroom to say that Father had been taken to hospital. I took the train down to look after them – it would only be a couple of days and it was nothing to panic about, just an irregular heartbeat. To make sure I could hear her if anything happened in the night, I made up the bed in the room which I had had as a child and which was unchanged at the end of the corridor. And Mother called out for me.

'*Ach, wie sehe ich aus!* Look at me! How have I ended up like this?' she moaned.

I tried to get her to sit up a little higher in the bed, put a pillow at her back and brushed her hair, which was thin and greasy with sweat. I carefully washed her face, and she asked for her perfume from the bedside drawer, and then I peeled an apple and cut it into thin slices, which I managed to get down her. She even drank a beer. And now her catheter was full, and I changed it, punctured the bag in the bathroom and had to clean up.

I would have given my life for hers, but she did not want it, lying in bed, refusing to drink and refusing to eat. It made no difference what I did, nothing helped, and I spent the evening putting acid-tasting sweets into Mother's mouth because they relieved the pain – she kept asking for her lemon drops – and slowly she turned the screw.

When I went to bed, she began to scream. I rushed into her bedroom. She was sitting bolt upright in the bed saying that she was going to be sick, she was going to be sick, and I ran to find a bowl, hearing her cursing the people, the country, me.

'Ach! Was seid ihr doch für Menschen? Pisseland, pisse, pisse, pisseland!'

And she threw it all up, the pills and the bits of apple and the beer I had got down her. I emptied the bowl a couple of times and sat by her bedside and said, 'Mother, you'll have to calm down now', and she lashed out at me – how could she calm down when she had vomited everywhere? I stroked her cheek and told a story to get her to forget herself and her pain and her body and to slowly lull her to sleep by talking.

Can you remember when we used to visit Grandmother, when we turned the corner where she lived? It was Ketten-hofweg number ... 108, wasn't it? I said the wrong number on purpose to get Mother's attention, and she corrected me, saying, *'Nein, 106,'* and I said that of course it was 106! And can you remember that the first thing you saw when you came into the hall was the post-boxes?

'Yes,' she replied. 'Of course.' And then you went in along a passageway to the left, I said, and came to a door with frosted glass, can you remember that? And when you rang, it made a buzzing noise, and Grandmother would let us in. We would go up the stairs – now what was she called, the woman who lived on the first floor, the Jewess?

'Frau Badrian,' Mother said with a snort.

And I said that, yes, that's what her name was. She was nice, and then one storey further up and we were at Grand-mother's. Can you remember the smell? There was such a comforting, cosy smell in the hall – and the glass door that shivered when you opened it to go into her living room.

It was a fine room, elegant, and we would eat dinner, and I loved Grandmother's cooking. Can you remember her kitchen? It was small, and her pots and pans were old, and the casserole was over a hundred years old?

Ja, wir haben immer auf unsere Sachen aufgepasst,' said Mother.

Yes, I said, you certainly did look after the family's things. And then I asked whether she could remember the view from the balcony in the bedroom that looked out onto the courtyard where the pension was – Pension Gölz. There was an Alsatian that was always barking and a large tree – a chestnut, wasn't it?

'They were chestnuts to eat,' Mother said. *'Esskastanien.* They don't have them in Dänemark'. I continued the tour, telling her how walking up Kettenhofweg you went past the house where the mad lady lived who collected all kinds of rubbish and made a huge tip in her front garden.

'Yes,' said Mother. 'I sat once beside her in the tram and she stank.' And I said that she would never move, would she?

'Nein,' she replied.

'Can you remember,' I asked, 'the name of the big street you got to, where the trams went?'

'Bockenheimer Landstraße.'

I whooped.

Yes! That's what it was called. And then you walked across the zebra crossing and there was a baker's – I loved Pfannkuchen – and around the corner a small, dark stationer's with biros, exercise books and paper of all colours.

There was a young lady who ran it – and what was the name of the street you got to, the big street that led all the way to Opernplatz?

'Goethestraße,' said Mother, and I said, Wow, you've got a good memory! And can you remember the ruins of the opera? Mother said that it wasn't so bad that it couldn't be rebuilt, and I said yes – and so we came to Palmengarten, the large park, where there was a lake you could take a boat on, and I was so happy there that I rowed all day long. There was a palm house, which was huge and made of nothing but glass and it was as hot as the tropics and humid and full of palms and there was a wishing well – and can you remember the playground?

'Yes,' Mother said and opened her eyes and looked at me with that cold, steely gaze that I had been afraid of all my life. 'And can you remember what happened?'

Yes, I said. I was playing in the climbing frame, which was shaped like an aeroplane, and I was flying across the water and refused to land before I had reached America.

'And then?' asked Mother, and I felt ashamed and answered that she had waited and waited and contracted pneumonia and almost died.

'Exactly,' Mother said with an unpleasant smile, and I knew that it would be now, and that I had reached the end of the story and she had not fallen asleep.

She was awake, and it was the other woman in Mother before me now, looking through her eyes and pointing at the sweets on the bedside table.

'Who put those sweets there?' she asked.

It was awful. I couldn't breathe, my chest contracted.

'I did.'

'What are they doing there?' she asked. 'Take them away!'

I went out into the kitchen with them and returned. She was scowling.

'Where is that little box?'

'Which box?'

'That little box with sweets,' she snapped. 'Where is it? *Wo? Wo?*'

Then I understood.

'But I took it away just now because you told me to,' I said, 'and because the sweets had melted in the heat of the bedroom.'

'Where is it?' she asked, her voice brittle and sharp, and I was forced to admit it – I had thrown them out. She looked at me accusingly – and then got cramp in her legs and began to scream, and the night was spent comforting her and changing catheters because she wanted a fresh one even though the bag wasn't full, and I stank of my mother's urine and vomit.

The day after – I had not slept more than ten minutes at a stretch – Mother lay with her eyes half closed looking as though she was going to die at any moment. I helped her get her pills down. Her throat was dry, and there were a lot of pills, and it was painful. She had to eat something, and I asked if she wanted a little ice cream – it was like the one you could get in Lübeck that she loved.

'Nein!' she said. 'Danish ice cream is full of disgusting cream.'

She was ready to throw up at the very thought. No, that Italian sorbet you could buy in Germany, now that was ice cream! I said I'd be happy to fetch some sorbet for her, and she said, 'In Dänemark they cannot make sorbet. They put cream in it,' and then she wanted to be changed, and I took the bag and emptied it down the toilet and fell asleep on the floor.

Mother was shouting, and I woke and rushed in to her. She was lying there shrieking, 'It's my bag! It's my bladder!' She was pulling at the catheter. 'Where is it? Where is it? Give it to me!' And she ripped the duvet aside and spread her legs, pulling at her underpants and showing me her sex where the tube from the catheter ended.

'Here it is! It is here and it is hot,' she said, and her eyes dilated and madness and evil shone from them.

'Stop this now, Mother,' I begged her, pleading. 'Won't you stop, please? There is nothing the matter. Won't you, please?'

And she screamed, '*Nein!* What are you thinking of? It is my bag! It's my bladder! You are an evil, evil boy! *Du bist ein böser Junge, nein!*'

With that she sat upright in the bed and took the water bottle and the glass from the bedside table and poured and gulped it down and poured a fresh one and drank, looking at me all the time, her face contorted, and I couldn't bear it any longer and ran out of the bedroom and down to the living room, terrified that Mother would come after me with her bad leg and kill me. I tried to ring the nurse at emergency but they were engaged. I left a message asking for help on the answerphone and had just put down the receiver, when Mother screamed from up in the bedroom, 'Ahhhhh! Knud! Knud!'

I ran upstairs. It stank, and I knew right away that it had happened. She lay on the bed looking like a skeleton in the foetal position, bent and bony – and I reached out to feel the pulse in her throat, and my hand withdrew automatically with a shock because it had encountered that most terrible thing of all, a corpse. Mother had become a thing, had been taken over by nature, which was rotting in her. Her mouth was open, her eyes were open and black and stared at me from far, far away. I could not understand that she was dead and I held her hand and stroked her cheek, her hair. I talked to her as though she were still alive – *'Süsse Mutti, ich hab' dich so lieb.'* As I told her I loved her, I almost thought her lips moved a little, and I put my ear to her mouth. Her breath had the sweetness of death. A sudden horror shot through me. She was going to pass on the name Papa Schneider had whispered to her, was going to tell it to me! I put my hands to my ears and did not want to hear it, shaking my head and looking at Mother. Her face was a petrified scream.

There was nothing peaceful about her death. Mother died a painful, tormented and miserable death. I rang the police, and the doctor arrived and pronounced her in rigor mortis, asking me about the circumstances in order to ensure that no crime had been committed. There had, I told him, but it was a long, long time ago – and then he completed the death certificate. Hildegard Lydia Voll Romer Jørgensen, I said, stressing the Romer. I asked him to allow her to stay where she was for a while. He nodded and left, and I sat at her bedside holding a wake all night long, talking with her, speaking to myself and swearing I would take revenge.

In the morning I rang the hospital, told Father and brought him home. He went in to see Mother. I made up a bed for him in the guest room, and we sat down at the dining table. I tried to hold his hand and comfort him and talk to him, but he was not to be comforted or talked to. He had nothing to say. At some point I rang the undertaker.

'Who are you ringing? What are you doing?' Father asked.

I didn't know what to say and just did it all as discreetly as I could to be free of his constant objections, and the undertaker arrived dressed in black.

His hands were shaking. He was clearly nervous. He took out a folder with the range of coffins – I pointed at the one without a cross – and the urns – I chose the simple one – and the obituary notices – I wanted the largest. And Father ruined it all. He said no to everything, kept asking what the point was and telling me that that was enough now. In the end I arranged for them to come and fetch her as late as possible, which meant at four o'clock.

The day passed then with Father, who complained about the slightest thing – the tea was too weak, it was too strong, and why had I taken the newspaper up into the sitting room with me, and who had moved the papers on the table.

'Not those plates! And what are the silver knives doing in the dishwasher?' No, I need not make a bite of lunch, and no, he didn't want any cake, and the undertaker arrived on the dot and rang the bell. They set up the coffin in the sitting room and asked us to let them get on with it. We went into my old room, and Father started sobbing, making the strangest noises and sounding like a hollow box, and I couldn't stand it, and now they were carrying her down.

Someone knocked at the door, and Father and I went down into the sitting room. Mother lay in the white coffin – they had put it where the Christmas tree usually stood – I laid her little pillow under her head, and Father started poking irritably at a ball of fluff in the carpet with his stick and then pointed at the table.

'What's that?' he asked.

I didn't understand and asked what he meant by 'What's that?'

'That,' he said, 'that thing lying there. What is it? What's it doing there? And who put it there?'

It was a bag of tea that I had put on the table. I removed it and then took my place in front of the coffin and stood with my arm around Father's shoulders until at last he spoke.

'I wonder what the time is now? When's the vicar coming?'

'But Father, they are only waiting for us to give the word,' I said, 'and then they'll carry her out.' And I fetched in the undertaker, and he screwed the lid down, and the assistant came in and they carried the coffin out to the hearse.

It was an afternoon of cloudless, blue sky. A half-moon hung up there, and the undertaker bowed stiffly. They rolled slowly away, the black car with the white coffin, turning the corner, and I looked up at the moon and promised myself that I would think of her every time I saw it hanging in the sky by day.

We went inside. The whole house smelt of corpse. I drew back the curtains and opened the doors and windows to air it out. Father objected, and I asked if we couldn't have some fresh air for a few minutes, but he wasn't having any of it and flew into a rage. Once the worst of the smell had gone, I shut the house up again and we sat down. I asked about the obituary notice, and Father said that it was no one else's business. I tried to explain that without one it would be as though she had never existed and was neither dead nor alive, as if the whole thing had never happened. He threw up his hands and shook his head.

Father had always said no whenever I wanted to do anything, and now he was against me putting a notice in the paper saying 'Our Beloved'. He didn't want me to use the word 'Beloved' or 'Dear' – a load of nonsense, he said. And I drafted an obituary for him with nothing but facts and showed it to him.

'Look, Father, is that what you want? She is no one, nothing – she is an object, a couple of dates – it's as though she died and had no one and nothing at all.' And he said no, and what was the point, and I was ready to burst into tears.

In the end I gave up and did it for myself and without asking his permission. I racked my brains to think what I should write, what it should say. I ended up with three little words, written under her name and the dates of her birth and death. They said it all. *O süßes Lied*. They came from Rilke's *Liebeslied*, which speaks of how on the violin the bow brings together two strings to make a single note, and we were one in the most innocent, most senseless purity of music. It was as clear as the black border round a mourning card, and I drove up to the undertaker, where I sat and went through it with him to make sure that he made no mistakes – I would break down if there was any mistake. I pointed out the German *ß* sign, which was the most important and most difficult letter of them all, saying that it was the German *sz*, and asked whether he knew what that was. He nodded, and I asked once again whether he was sure, and he nodded, and I said it over and over until it was hammered into place.

When the newspaper came, the *Berlingske Tidende*, I ran down to the hall to get it and turned to the obituaries, and there it was, Mother's – *O süßes Lied* – and it read *O Sübes Lied* with a capital letter and misspelt with a *b*. He hadn't known what a *ß* was, had paid no attention at all – and my head spun, for everything was and would always be in vain. Nothing would ever succeed.

There could be no question of having a German hymn, said the priest, and *Jeg ved en dejlig have* was not a hymn and wouldn't do. I would have to talk to the sexton about getting a piano for the funeral, but he was very doubtful as it would first have to be moved and then be tuned and that would cost 500 kroner. The church was empty, and all the hymns were played too fast to get it over quickly, and the priest did not say it, didn't say 'Romer', despite my having asked him to – 'and Hildegard ... Jørgensen lived through the horrors of the war, and Hildegard ... Jørgensen came to Denmark in 1950.'

The Danish flag hung at half mast outside Klosterkirken, and the undertaker was waiting as we left the church and handed me an envelope containing the cards of those who had sent flowers. They were all from me. Then I struggled out to the car with Father, holding an umbrella over him because it was raining, and he said, 'What are you doing?' and 'Do stop that, will you!' We drove out to the church-yard with Father complaining all the way.

'Watch where you're going! Not that way. Look at the way you're driving! Listen, where do you thinking you're going?'

I took the route along the seafront looking out across the sound, and then we were at Østre Kirkegård, walking towards the grave where Farmor and Grandfather were buried, and the gravedigger laid Mother's urn in the ground and covered it with earth.

Father didn't want to have a gravestone. It was no one else's business. Why did they need to know who was buried there? It was nothing to do with them! There was nothing – just the black and white chippings and a plaque with a number. Then we came home, and I made coffee and laid out two cups and saucers on the dining table. We didn't say a word. I covered my face in my hands and burst into tears and cried and cried for Mother and Father, for everything that had happened and for the immeasurable loss of everything you hold most dear, and then it was over.

I went into my bedroom and opened the drawer. It was all still in there – the shells, the fossilized sea urchins, the old ham sandwiches, the fulgurites and the marbles – but I was looking for the fragments of grenade that I had been given by Uncle Helmut. I pieced them together one by one until I found myself sitting there with a complete Russian hand grenade, just as he had said. I filled it full of everything I had inside me – the grief and the despair and the fury – and then I fitted the detonator and walked up onto Højbroen to look out across Nykøbing from the bridge one last time. Then I pulled out the pin and hurled it as far out as I possibly could and closed my eyes and stuck a finger in each ear.